P9-CRH-200

GET ALL THIS FREE

WITH JUST ONE PROOF OF PURCHASE:

◆ **Hotel Discounts** up to 60% at home and abroad

$50 VALUE

◆ **Travel Service -** Guaranteed lowest published airfares plus 5% cash back on tickets ◆ **$25 Travel Voucher** ◆ **Sensuous Petite Parfumerie** collection ◆ **Insider Tips Letter** with sneak previews of upcoming books

You'll get a FREE personal card, too. It's your passport to all these benefits— and to even more great gifts & benefits to come!

There's no club to join. No purchase commitment. No obligation.

SD-PP6A

Enrollment Form

☐ *Yes!* I WANT TO BE A *Privileged Woman.*
Enclosed is one *PAGES & PRIVILEGES™* Proof of
Purchase from any Harlequin or Silhouette book currently for
sale in stores (Proofs of Purchase are found on the back pages
of books) and the store cash register receipt. Please enroll me
in *PAGES & PRIVILEGES™*. Send my Welcome Kit and FREE
Gifts -- and activate my FREE benefits -- immediately.

More great gifts and benefits to come.

_____

NAME (please print)

_____

ADDRESS   **APT. NO**

_____

CITY   **STATE**   **ZIP/POSTAL CODE**

**NO CLUB!
NO COMMITMENT!**
*Just one purchase brings
you great Free Gifts and
Benefits!*

Please allow 6-8 weeks for delivery. Quantities are limited. We reserve the right to
substitute items. Enroll before October 31, 1995 and receive one full year of benefits.

Name of store where this book was purchased_____

Date of purchase_____

Type of store:

   ☐ Bookstore ☐ Supermarket ☐ Drugstore

   ☐ Dept. or discount store (e.g. K-Mart or Walmart)

   ☐ Other (specify)_____

Which Harlequin or Silhouette series do you usually read?

_____

Complete and mail with one Proof of Purchase and store receipt to:

U.S.: *PAGES & PRIVILEGES™*, P.O. Box 1960, Danbury, CT 06813-1960

Canada: *PAGES & PRIVILEGES™*, 49-6A The Donway West, P.O. 813,
North York, ON M3C 2E8

▼ DETACH HERE AND MAIL TODAY! ▼

"Looking Good, Baaaby!"

Lost in reverie, Cat jumped a mile at the Bronco driver's hollering and horn blaring. But not for nothing had she survived and thrived in New York City.

"You rude, insolent, crazy man!" she shouted heatedly, shaking her fist. Whether the arrogant driver had heard or seen her, she didn't know. But she hoped he had; she hoped he knew that she had not appreciated his antics one bit! "I don't care if they *are* California *boys*, east, west, north or south—men are all alike."

Still fuming, Cat got into her Jeep and started it. It was not long before she spied the Bronco and its infuriating driver ahead of her, no longer going like a bat out of hell, but poking along at a snail's pace. She could see that the good-looking driver was now yakking on a cellular telephone.

At the sight, some devil seized Cat, and she stamped on the accelerator and jammed her hand on the horn as she whipped into the empty oncoming lane to pull alongside the Bronco.

"Hey, you! Eat dirt, you—you...*sodbuster!*"

Dear Reader,

It's not every month a *New York Times* bestselling writer joins the Desire family, so it's with great excitement that I get to announce that REBECCA BRANDEWYNE has become a part of Silhouette Books. Rebecca's *Wildcat* is not only a very special MAN OF THE MONTH, it's also her first full-length *contemporary* romance. You'll fall in love with rough and rugged oilman Morgan McCain as he spars with spirited Cat Devlin; and you'll never forget their passionate love story!

I'm equally thrilled about the rest of October's lineup. Award winner Cindy Gerard makes her Silhouette Desire debut with the sensuous Western *The Cowboy Takes A Lady*. And if you're a fan of BJ James, don't miss *A Wolf In The Desert*, book #3 in her MEN OF THE BLACK WATCH series.

And if you enjoy time travel—or even if you don't— you'll *love* Cathie Linz's *A Wife in Time*. Cathie's delightful dialogue and sexy stories are, well, *timeless*. Talented author Audra Adams brings us a dramatic story of powerful love and possible betrayal with *The Bachelor's Bride*.

Bringing you a *brand-new*, never-before-published writer is always a special moment for an editor, and I'm *very* enthusiastic about our PREMIERE author Christine Pacheco. Don't miss her first published book, *The Rogue and the Rich Girl*.

Silhouette Desire: we've got something for everyone! So enjoy…

Lucia Macro
Senior Editor

Please address questions and book requests to:
Silhouette Reader Service
U.S.: 3010 Walden Ave., P.O. Box 1325, Buffalo, NY 14269
Canadian: P.O. Box 609, Fort Erie, Ont. L2A 5X3

Rebecca Brandewyne
WILDCAT

SILHOUETTE *Desire*®
Published by Silhouette Books
America's Publisher of Contemporary Romance

For my editor,
Tara Gavin,
with heartfelt appreciation
for her faith, her friendship and her kindness.

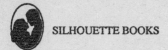

SILHOUETTE BOOKS

ISBN 0-373-05955-8

WILDCAT

REBECCA BRANDEWYNE

is a bestselling author of historical novels. Her stories consistently place on the bestseller lists, including the *New York Times* and *Publishers Weekly*. She was inducted into the *Romantic Times* Hall of Fame in 1988, and is the recipient of the *Romantic Times* Career Achievement Award (1991), *Affaire de Coeur*'s Golden Quill Award for Best Historical Romance and the Silver Pen Award.

Wildcat

Now, he was just a good ole country boy,
An outlaw, pure and wild,
While she was a red-headed city girl,
Not easily beguiled.
But opposites attract, it's often said—
And that proved true for them.
One glance, and he felt a longing for her,
And she the same for him.

Wildcat...it's a fire burning out of control.
Wildcat...it's two halves that are finally whole.

East met west on a dusty country road,
And sparks flew from the start,
Igniting a blaze untamped, untamed,
Deep in each other's heart.
They fought, they wrangled, they made up, but just
Could not break up the team,
Begun with a pair of bold, one-eyed jacks,
Then a dance to a dream.

Wildcat...it's a fire burning out of control.
Wildcat...it's the hand, the heart, and the soul.

One

Country Boy
Wichita, Kansas

Morgan McCain was an outlaw.

He had always been an outlaw, and he suspected he always would be an outlaw, cut from the same rough cloth as Waylon Jennings and Willie Nelson and all the rest whose heroes had always been cowboys and who had been born a century too late for Deadwood, Dodge City and Tombstone. Hell. Morgan had even arrived too late for the Cimarron Strip, when men had gambled at oil instead of cards, and the outlaws had all been wildcatters, betting that black gold would come gushing out of the rich, rolling prairie earth. Yes, those had been the days—and Morgan, much to his regret, had missed them. The only bronco he rode was a Ford; the closest he had ever come to a showdown at high noon was a Saturday-night brawl in some rowdy bar; and at the moment the oil business was not booming, but bust. Still, the fact remained that in his heart he was an outlaw, pure and simple.

That he was a throwback to the nineteenth century had not proved detrimental to Morgan's well-being, however. Rather, this characteristic had held him in good stead. For, from their winnings one night at a boisterous, back-room poker game straight out of a Western movie, he and his partner, Frank Devlin, had together started their business, the One-Eyed Jacks Oil & Gas Company, afterward somehow managing to hang on through the tough, lean years, when a lot of other oilmen had gone under. But although Morgan's initial gamble had paid off, it now appeared that his lucky streak had finally played out. Frank was unexpectedly dead of a heart attack, and the future of the corporation they had owned fifty-fifty was currently up in the air due to his last will and testament.

Frank's attorney, Richard Hollis, had refused even to hint at the document's contents until Frank's only living relative, his daughter, was informed of her father's death, and Morgan had not pressed the issue. Still, he felt certain Frank had willed his shares in the company to that only child, that snooty, ungrateful daughter who had not only left all her father's funeral arrangements up to Morgan, but who had not even bothered to show up at Frank's graveside service. Instead, upon being notified of her father's death, she had cabled instructions to both Frank's attorney and Morgan, informing them that she was out of the country and would be in touch with them when she returned.

Of course, it was not her fault that she had been abroad when Frank had died. Still, Morgan could not rid himself of the suspicion that Ms. Catherine Devlin had not cared two hoots in hell about her father—one of the finest men Morgan had ever known. Nor, as a result, did he think she was going to have the slightest bit of interest in the oil company he and Frank had worked so hard to build over the years. It was more than likely, Morgan thought as he stared morosely out his wide office window, that she would want to sell her father's shares as soon as possible, and Morgan was not sure that at the moment he could put together the necessary financing to buy her out. That left him with some pretty unappealing alternatives: he could attempt to sell his own shares in the company; he could waste his own time and money looking for another partner; he could resign himself to getting stuck with whatever investor Ms. Catherine Devlin wound up selling her shares to; or he could try to talk her into dissolving the corporation and liquidating its assets.

Morgan's mouth turned down sourly at the corners as he considered those options. Damn it! He was not about to throw away without a fight everything he and Frank had striven so hard to achieve. They had not scratched and clawed their way through the muck to strike oil, only to lose it all because of some big-city, Seven-Sisters woman from back East. Why Frank had always, in his generous heart, had a tender spot for that daughter of his, Morgan could not fathom. Not once had she ever deigned to come visit her father in Wichita, although Frank had on several occasions traveled to New York to see her, returning to sing her praises until Morgan, scowling, had made his apathy and annoyance plain, cutting Frank off in midsentence.

Frank had always shaken his head ruefully at that, claiming that Morgan, never having been a father himself, just would not and could not understand. That he, Frank, had been estranged from his daughter for so many years was regrettable, but their lack of contact could not be laid at Catherine's door. It was not her fault. Her mother, Julia Talbot, Frank's ex-wife, had filled the girl's head with bitter, spiteful tales against him and had coldly made it clear to both Cat and Frank that his presence was entirely unwelcome in the Talbot family mansion, to which Julia had returned following the divorce.

"I should have fought harder to stay in touch with Cat from the beginning," Frank had always insisted. "But back then, I was just a nobody struggling to make ends meet, while the Talbots had social standing and money. Naturally, they hired all the best lawyers to ensure that I had no rights whatsoever when it came to Cat. What could I do—me, Julia Talbot's one moment of youthful rebellion and indiscretion? I'd worked on the grounds of her daddy's estate before she and I eloped, and her old man subsequently fired me for seducing his innocent little girl. It didn't matter that she was neither innocent nor little, nor that she had shamelessly flung herself at me, claiming she didn't care about the consequences—a lie she soon came to regret, once she learned what it meant to be poor. No, I didn't stand a chance against her daddy and his attorneys, and I knew it, so I just walked away and never looked back, until Cat was old enough to make her own decisions. Cat's not to blame for that."

In his heart, Morgan had sensed the truth of that declaration. Still, he had never found it within himself to forgive Ms. Catherine Devlin for her indifference toward her father. It galled Morgan no end that now, because of Frank's soft heart, Catherine was in a position to destroy the One-Eyed Jacks Oil & Gas Company.

Muttering angrily to himself, he abruptly swung his booted feet down from his oak credenza, swiveled in his big, burgundy leather chair and stood. It was plain to him that in his ill mood he was not going to accomplish anything in the office today. Despite the fact that he had arrived at the crack of dawn that morning, his massive oak, antique rolltop desk was still piled high with unsigned contracts, unread letters and unreturned messages. Trailing from his leather-bound wastebasket was a long, crumpled paper chain of oil derricks, which he did not even remember cutting out earlier. Glancing at the heirloom grandfather clock towering against one parchment-colored wall, he saw that he had been staring out the office window now for more than an hour, oblivious of the swans and ducks that floated lazily on the winding waterway beyond—normally a tranquilizing sight—and of the resonate chiming of the clock itself, marking the passage of time. Grabbing his black Stetson hat from the brass coatrack that stood in one corner, he jammed it on his head, then ripped open his office door with such force that his secretary, Mrs. Whittingdale, seated at her desk just outside, jumped.

"Whitty, cancel any appointments I have this afternoon. I'm taking the rest of the day off," Morgan growled, uncomfortably aware of how surly he sounded, but unable to summon a politer tone.

Fortunately, Whitty, as he had nicknamed her within days of having hired her, was an older, motherly sort who had been with him for many years, so she was long accustomed to his bad temper.

"Yes, Morgan," she replied smoothly to his broad back as he stamped past her, for she saw no reason to agitate him further by announcing that upon determining his mood earlier that morning, she'd already taken the liberty of clearing his calendar for the day. As his and the late Frank Devlin's personal secretary, Whitty was privy to every business detail at the One-Eyed Jacks Oil & Gas Company, so she knew that with the company's future now wholly uncertain, Morgan had good cause for his current disposition—besides which, he had taken Frank's death pretty hard. "It's too beautiful a day to be cooped up inside, anyway," she declared sympathetically. "It'll do you good to get away for a while. You work too hard, Morgan. You always have."

His only response was a scornful snort that left Whitty shaking her head sadly and clucking with distress as he vanished into the hallway. *He ought to be married and raising a family,* she thought, not for the first time. But once bitten, twice shy, and Veronica Havers, the one woman Morgan had ever been serious about, had dumped him in the end for a cool, sophisticated financial investor with old money.

Once outside in the parking lot, Morgan climbed furiously into his Bronco. After slamming the door and tossing his Stetson onto the seat beside him, he punched the key into the ignition and started up the engine with a roar, gunning it once or twice before, spinning the steering wheel and burning rubber, he lurched out onto Woodlawn, unconsciously heading north toward the country, as he always did when he needed to be alone for a while.

His one clear thought as he did so was how much he would like to have just ten minutes of Ms. Catherine Devlin's precious time, so he could give her a piece of his mind, tell her exactly what he thought of her—the stuck-up, hardhearted witch!

Two

City Girl

When Catherine Devlin jerked awake from the fitful doze into which she had fallen, she was dazed from jet lag and lack of sleep and disoriented by her unfamiliar surroundings. Her first thought as she stared through the sun-warmed window her cheek was pressed against was that she must still be asleep and dreaming—a bizarre, disjointed dream in which she had become a pioneer woman, braving the frontier. Upon gradually realizing she was awake and aware, however, her second thought was that, like the bewildered heroine of some time-travel novel, she had somehow while she napped been zapped and transported back in time. For what met her startled gaze was a small cluster of old buildings that belonged not to the twentieth century and a modern city, but to the nineteenth century and a Wild West town in which Wyatt Earp and John Henry "Doc" Holliday would have been perfectly at home.

Good heavens. It's finally happened. I've snapped at last, Cat reflected with a strange sense of calm detachment. *I've gone clean off my rocker, over the edge, off the deep end, out of my head....* Funny, until now she had never thought about how many ways there were to say you had lost your hold on reality, on sanity, and now dwelled in the chaotic realm of the lunatic, the deranged. But that was surely what had befallen her, she mused as she stared at the grill in front of her face, the rusty iron fretwork that separated her from the man in white who must certainly even now be driving her to some sanatorium.

Slowly straightening from her slumped position, Cat ground the heels of her palms into her bleary eyes, red rimmed from fatigue and weeping. At least she had the use of her hands, was not confined by a straitjacket.

"You all right, ma'am? You seem awful tired, if you don't mind my saying so. You must have had a long flight. Funny thing, how we can fly all over the world and even put a man on the moon, but nobody appears to be able to find a cure for jet lag. You ought to be in bed, ma'am. But you *did* tell me to take the scenic route." The kindly tone of the driver, a young college student dressed in a white T-shirt and blue jeans, turned slightly defensive at the end.

All at once, Cat remembered where she was—and why— and the sorrow that had threatened to overwhelm her the past few days rose anew to haunt her.

"Yes, that's right, I did," she replied quietly to the driver, who was glancing at her with concern in his rearview mirror. "I've never been to Wichita before, and I wanted to see something of the city." The minute this confession left her mouth, she silently cursed herself for a fool.

She might not have lost her mind, but she clearly was not thinking straight all the same. She had been under such a terrible strain lately, and her father's death had been the crowning blow. One of her cardinal rules for survival was never to tell a taxi driver she was new in town. Now he un-

doubtedly saw her as an easy mark and would meander all
over the city in order to rack up charges on the meter. Still,
Cat was too weary to protest, as she normally would have
done, her long experience with New York City cabbies
making other cities' taxi drivers appear wholly unintimi-
dating.

"Are they shooting a film here...a Western?" she asked
curiously, indicating the buildings that had so startled and
confused her moments before.

"What? Oh, no, ma'am. That's Cowtown...old Wichita. Among other things, Munger House, the city's first
story-and-a-half house, is there, and the original jail. Wyatt
Earp was a policeman here back in those days, you know,"
the driver announced, eliciting an unexpected smile from
Cat as she remembered her thought just moments ago
about the famous lawman.

Encouraged by her smile, the driver continued to point
out sights along the way as he wound through the city and
its riverside parks, indeed obviously taking the scenic route.
They passed the Mid-America All-Indian Center, a mu-
seum. Botanica, a botanical garden. Like a tour guide, he
was a veritable font of information and kept up a stream of
congenial chatter Cat only half heard. Although she made
appropriate polite responses, her mind was now focused on
collecting her thoughts as she prepared herself to step into
her father's life here in Wichita, feeling both guilt and grief
that she should do so only at his death. How horribly ironic
that she had planned on visiting him here this summer, only
to learn a few days ago that she had left it too late.

Informed of her father's death, being unable to get to
Wichita in time for his funeral, Cat need not have come
here at all. Frank Devlin's attorney, Richard Hollis, had
told her that her actual physical presence was not necessary for the legalities to be handled. Arrangements could be
made for a realtor to sell her father's house, for its fur-
nishings to be auctioned off beforehand at an estate sale

and for his vehicles to be sold. If she wished, Morgan McCain, her father's partner, would even pack up her father's personal belongings and send them to her. Still, once back from Europe, Cat had, from New York's La Guardia Airport, caught the first flight bound for Wichita, damning the expense and not caring that time-consuming connections and exhausting layovers had been required. Why she had come, she still did not know—except that she had felt she somehow owed it to her father.

By now they had left downtown Wichita behind, and the driver was explaining that the neighborhood in which her father had lived, Vickridge, had been named after the estate of a local oilman, Jack A. Vickers, who, back in the early, booming days of oil, had founded the Vickers Petroleum Company. There were a lot of oil companies in Wichita, it appeared. Even Koch—as famous for its bitter family feuds and Bill Koch's 1992 win of the America's Cup as for its industries—had headquarters here. Then all too soon, it seemed, the taxi was pulling into the half-circle driveway before her father's house.

For a long moment Cat just sat in the cab, staring at the huge Tudor home and wishing her mother were here to see how high "that penniless, worthless bum Frank Devlin, your father," had climbed. A lump rose in Cat's throat and tears stung her eyes. Her heart filled to overflowing with love for and pride in her father.

You done good, Dad, she thought, hoping that some way, somewhere, her silent words reached him. *You done real good.*

She had her father's keys, express mailed to her by his attorney in case she decided to make the trip to Wichita, as well as various items of information that included how to deactivate the alarm system. So once the taxi had driven away, she turned the house key in the lock and pushed open the heavy, solid oak front door. After entering the proper code sequence to shut off the alarm, Cat carried her luggage inside.

She knew at once, as, from the marble-floored foyer, she surveyed her beautiful, tasteful surroundings, that the house's interior had been decorated by a professional. Frank Devlin had been a plain, honest, hardworking man of humble beginnings. Unlike her mother, he had never known a Rembrandt from a reproduction, Baccarat from cut glass or Porthault from percale. Once she had got to know him, Cat had always found that oddly endearing. Every time they had ever passed a street vendor in New York, she had had to haul her father away, scolding him good-naturedly and explaining that the hucksters weren't *really* selling Rolex watches for twenty bucks apiece, but cheap counterfeits or knockoffs.

"But, Cat, the last time I was here I bought a damned good umbrella from one of these guys!" her father had always protested, his eyes twinkling with mischief.

"Umbrellas are different, Dad," she had invariably answered, shaking her head ruefully. "It's a public service to sell decent umbrellas in New York—because you can never get a cab here when it's raining!"

Now, as these memories of her father assailed her, Cat could not help but smile through her tears. She almost expected to see his tall, handsome, silver-haired figure striding toward her, a big bear of a man, larger than life—and with a heart even larger still. But the house was empty, bereft of her father himself, if not his presence. The smell of the cigars he had smoked, of the cologne he had worn, lingered in the rooms she gradually explored one by one, until she came to the last room. *Her* room. She knew it instinctively when she saw it, for all her favorite things were here: an old canopy bed she had once admired in an antique store in New York during a shopping spree with her father; a nightstand stacked high with books Frank Devlin would never have read and compact discs he would never have listened to; a dresser filled with Victorian perfume flacons, which she collected.

"Oh, Dad," she whispered aloud in the thoughtfully, so obviously caringly prepared room, her heart breaking, her voice catching on a ragged sob. "I'm sorry...so sorry for all the lost, wasted years...so sorry I didn't get here in time! I should never have listened to all of Mother's tales about you! But I never realized until I was older how selfish, self-centered and bitter she was. I should never have worked so hard at my job, either, been so damned busy climbing the corporate ladder that I had too little time for my family and friends. I should have *made* time! I should have come here while you were still alive...."

Worst of all was the letter Cat found later that evening in her father's study, once she had begun the task of sorting through some of the papers in his desk. It was a loving, enthusiastic missive written to her, detailing all the things he planned for them to do together this summer, when she would at last make the long-awaited visit to Wichita. She had never received the letter, of course; her father's sudden heart attack had killed him before he had had a chance to mail it to her or even address an envelope.

Earlier, during her foray into the kitchen, Cat had discovered nothing edible in her father's big, built-in Sub-Zero refrigerator. For supper, therefore, she had made do with ordering a pizza, which she had learned, much to her frustration, was the only food anybody delivered in Wichita—and that probably only because the Carney brothers, Dan and Frank, had, in a little hole-in-the-wall building here, started what had eventually grown into the worldwide corporation of Pizza Hut. Now, as she read her father's words, the bite of sausage and pepperoni on a thin crust that she had just eaten stuck in her throat, tight with emotion, and the taste of the hot, fresh pizza was suddenly like cardboard on her tongue. After slowly folding up the letter, she laid her head on her father's desk and wept for a very long time.

When she was all cried out, Cat finally understood what had compelled her to come to Wichita: she wanted to do all those things her father had planned for them and about which he had written to her. She wanted to be a part of his life, just as he had been a part of hers. In that moment her decision about her immediate future was made.

"I'm going to stay here…at least for a while, Dad," she said aloud, as though her father sat with her in his study. And in a way, perhaps he did, she thought as she played idly with the things on his desk: his wooden box of cigars, his gold letter opener, his gold pen-and-pencil set, a small brass oil derrick he had evidently used as a paperweight. "I don't know how I'll do here, a big-city girl like me in this 'Cowtown' of yours. I suppose they don't deliver groceries here, either! But I'm going to give Wichita the chance you wanted me to, even so." Cat paused for a moment, considering that declaration. Then she continued.

"The truth is it'll do me good to be away from New York for a while, seeing as how my life's in such a shambles at the moment. You see, I've fallen off the corporate ladder, Dad, fallen long and hard. Right before you—before you…died, Spence and I had a dreadful argument in Europe during our buying trip for the firm, and well, the upshot of it was that I not only broke off our engagement, but in retaliation, he fired me."

Spencer Kingsley, her fiancé, had been her boss at the import-export firm where she had worked. He had been attracted to her from the very first day she had walked into his office, but in the beginning Cat had been wary of mixing business with pleasure, of having an affair with her employer. Spence, however, had pursued her with all the relentless determination he had used to pursue a prized order for the firm, and in the end she had allowed her reservations to be overcome, herself to be persuaded that his intentions toward her were both honorable and serious. And they had been. He had wanted to marry her.

But from the minute he had got his three-carat-diamond engagement ring on her finger, Spence had behaved as though he had owned her; and gradually, Cat had come to recognize that he was as dictatorial and disapproving as her mother, forever preaching about "knowing the right people, moving in the right circles and being seen at the right places." Her mother had adored him, exclaiming effusively—*gushing* was actually the word that had applied to her mother's behavior, Cat thought now—about Spence's impeccable background, breeding and money, how well he "fit in" with the Talbot family, how "wise" Cat was not to make a terrible mistake by running off with someone like her father, someone "not of their class."

"I was so young and foolish when I married that penniless, worthless bum Frank Devlin, your father," Julia Talbot had insisted, her carefully lipsticked mouth twisting in a wry grimace. "I thought the things with which I'd been reared and which I'd come to expect didn't matter. I thought Frank and I could live on love alone. What a stupid notion that was, I soon learned! After marriage, love goes right out the window, dear...you'll see. You'll be glad then of the rewards and comforts that Spence's position and money will bring."

"That's when I first realized that if I married Spence, I was going to turn into Mother, Dad," Cat added, continuing her one-sided conversation in the shadowy study. "You were right about Spence—he *was* as dull as ditch water! And there *was* some vital spark missing in our relationship. But if I ever *do* find that certain something with some certain someone, I think I'll know it now, Dad."

As she stood and reached to turn off the banker's lamp on her father's desk, Cat spied his letter, lying where she had laid it earlier on the black leather blotter. The missive had come unfolded, and now his last words to her leapt up at her again from the page: *P.S. I can hardly wait for you to meet Morgan! My two "wildcats"—together at last!*

"You trying to tell me something, Dad?" she inquired, her eyebrows arching faintly at what she now perceived as his sheer impudence, even from the grave.

It was surely only her imagination, but as Cat left the study, she could have sworn she heard her father's laughter echo softly behind her in the dark, empty room.

Three

East Meets West

Morgan had left the city limits behind. Now he barreled north down a dirt road along which farmers' fields seemed to stretch endlessly for miles—acres and acres of wheat, corn and milo, mostly. The green-and-gold fields of grain were a beautiful sight. The wheat, especially, was like an amber sea in the sunlight, its feathery heads rippling gently like waves in the wind that stirred the prairie. Morgan's gaze, however, took in only the ugly beam pumps that sparsely dotted the earth, the pumping units of some standing still, motionless, while others churned steadily, sucking up the oil, the black gold, that lay deep beneath the surface.

He did not own the fields themselves, but he *did* hold the oil and gas leases on some of them—or, rather, the One-Eyed Jacks Oil & Gas Company did. So periodically, even though the corporation had maintenance men for the task, he drove out to various sites to assure himself that all machinery was working properly, that those beam pumps currently in operation were functioning as they ought. No matter how they scarred the earth, rising like an army of titanic, alien robots, Morgan found that the sight of the beam pumps always soothed his temper and filled him with pride. From nothing but a pair of jacks and a one-eyed ax-man, which had provided a winning hand at poker for each of them, he and Frank had built all of this, starting out as wildcatters—those who took chances on fields not previously known to harbor oil.

But Morgan possessed, as had Frank, an uncanny gut instinct about oil. It was as though he could smell it a mile away. Sometimes he had only to walk onto a field and he would know oil was there, lying deep beneath his booted feet, waiting to be freed, to come spewing out of the rich earth that yielded it.

"Drill here," he would say suddenly, quivering with excitement and anticipation, certain that were he a dowser, his divining rod would be shaking uncontrollably as it pointed toward the ground upon which he stood.

He proved right so much more often than wrong that even the geologists, baffled by his finding what had not appeared to them to be present, eventually ceased arguing with him, stopped holding up their education and training against Morgan McCain's "nose." The first time the crude had come gushing from the earth, he and Frank, shouting and laughing, had thrown their Stetsons high into the sky and had danced about like crazy men while the black gold rained upon them. Even now, the memory of that day was as clear in Morgan's mind as though it had happened only yesterday, and as always, the thought brought an irrepressible grin to his handsome, tanned face.

Adding to the gradual lightening of his dark mood was the fact that he had the windows of the Bronco rolled down, so the wind streamed exhilaratingly through the vehicle, and the radio, tuned to a country-and-western station, was playing his favorite good-time music. As he drove he banged one hand against the steering wheel in time to the beat, and now and then he sang along, too. His mama, before she had died, had surely never listened to this particular song, he thought, still grinning, or else she would never have let him grow up to be a cowboy, but would have made him become a doctor or a lawyer.

By now, despite all his troubles, Morgan's spirits had lifted so considerably that when he spied a striking young redheaded woman standing in the wheat field he was currently passing, he did not pause to wonder what she was doing out there, all by her lonesome self, or how his actions might affect her. Instead, he did the only thing any other red-blooded American cowboy would have done: he hollered out the window at her and laid on the horn—full blast.

Cat had not informed either her father's attorney, Richard Hollis, or her father's partner, Morgan McCain, that she was coming to Wichita; nor had she yet notified them of her presence in their city. She had wanted a day or so to rest, to come to grips with the loss of her father and to get her bearings, especially since she had decided to stay awhile. So the following morning, when she awoke, she determined that the first thing she needed to do was shop for groceries so she wouldn't turn into a Ninja Turtle from a steady diet of pizza. Also, she needed to locate a bank, where, with her traveler's checks, she planned to open a checking account.

Finding the two closets in her bedroom empty save for several padded satin hangers her father had thoughtfully provided, she finished unpacking her luggage, having removed only the bare essentials last night. She was glad the dresser and armoire were also empty, because such had been her haste in getting to Wichita that she had come straight here, carrying with her every piece of luggage she had taken to Europe, never having bothered to unpack between the two trips. Since the European business venture had lasted three weeks, Cat had plenty of clothes with her, and she was confident she could buy anything she might lack.

An invigorating shower washed away the remaining vestiges of her jet lag and weariness, after which she donned a matching set of silky, lacy underwear, a pair of Calvin Klein jeans and a simple green knit shell. Then she slipped a pair of heeled sandals onto her bare feet. She wore minimal makeup: black mascara to darken her long, thick lashes; fawn-colored eyeshadow to emphasize her slightly slanted green eyes; pink blush to highlight her fine cheekbones and porcelain skin; wine red lipstick to accentuate her generous, sultry mouth. After a quick brushing, her dark red hair hung shining and free, falling to just below her shoulders.

Grabbing her purse and her father's keys, Cat made her way to the garage. There she discovered a brand-new Jeep Cherokee Limited, a classic Cadillac convertible and a sleek speedboat. Living in New York, she had not needed a car, so it had been a long while since she had driven. The Jeep looked sturdy and practical, so she attempted to open the garage door behind it, tugging with increasing frustration when the door refused to budge. Finally, feeling like the world's biggest fool, she discovered in the Jeep itself a remote control for the automatic garage-door opener, which she had not previously noticed.

"Presto, chango," she commented dryly as she pressed the button and the garage door rose easily.

After backing out the driveway, she wound slowly through Vickridge, taking time to familiarize herself with the Jeep and with the neighborhood, noting street signs so she could find her way home again. Reaching a four-lane main street that she observed was named Rock Road, she turned right, not trusting her driving ability enough to turn left instead, across two lanes of oncoming traffic. A few blocks later she pulled into a gas station, bought a map of Wichita and inquired of the attendant about the area's grocery stores and banks. To her amazement and delight, the grocery store he recommended, Dillons, proved to be a "superstore" that boasted not only groceries, but also meat and fish markets, Chinese takeout, discount items, a pharmacy, a post office, a dry cleaner, a shoe-repair drop, a branch library and a branch bank.

Cat transacted her business at the bank first, then did her shopping. By the time she was finished, her grocery cart looked to her as though she were preparing for a siege. She was not used to being able to buy so much all in one place at one time. In an hour she was back home again, ruing her impulsiveness when she had to unload the Jeep, carry all the sacks inside and put everything away by herself. But then she realized she would not have to do this every other day, making several small trips a week to the market as she had often had to do in New York to supplement her usual delivery of groceries.

"So, okay, Dad," Cat conceded aloud with a wry smile, as she deposited milk, eggs and cheese in the refrigerator. "I'll admit I wouldn't have supposed it, but you were right—apparently there *are* some advantages to living in this Cowtown of yours. And as you kept badgering me to do, I've taken a step in broadening my horizons. For the first time in a long while, I drove a car today—not very well, I confess, but still, I drove it. And I managed to find my way around town a little, too. And guess what? In just a minute I'm going to go back out again. I want to see some of these oil wells and wheat fields you talked about, Dad, some of this prairie you loved so much that you called it God's country."

There had been a map in her father's desk, with marks on it to indicate the locations of various oil wells belonging to the One-Eyed Jacks Oil & Gas Company. So, armed with that and her city map, Cat, true to her word, resolutely headed back out in the Jeep once she had emptied all the grocery sacks.

And that was how she came to be standing alone in a wheat field when Morgan McCain passed her in his Bronco, grinning and yelling out the window at her and blaring the horn for all he was worth.

Lost in reverie, Cat jumped a mile, catching her heel on a clod of dirt, so her ankle twisted beneath her and she fell smack upon the curvaceous posterior that, among other attributes, had prompted Morgan's hollering and horn blaring in the first place. But not for nothing had Cat survived and even thrived in New York.

"You damned rude, insolent, crazy man!" she shouted heatedly, shaking her fist at the Bronco, which sped on by, trailing a cloud of dust in its wake. Whether its arrogant driver had heard or seen her, she did not know. But she fiercely hoped he had; she hoped he knew she had not appreciated his damned fool antics one bit! "Oh, Jeez Louise, why didn't you wear more-sensible shoes, Cat—some hiking boots or something if you were going to be traipsing around out here in the boondocks?" she chided herself after a moment as, gingerly reaching beneath her, she drew forth a small clump of sharp cockleburs that had been stabbing her in the behind and that now pricked her fingers, as well.

With anger and disgust she tossed the cockleburs away, realizing as she did so that some large black bug had taken advantage of her current position to begin crawling up her jeans. Screeching and swiping wildly at the insect, Cat scrambled to her feet, wincing at the pain as her weight bore down upon her injured ankle. Cursing and muttering to herself every step of the way, she limped toward the Jeep, which she had parked on the grassy verge of the road.

"Damned grinning lunatic!" she groused. "Probably escaped from some asylum." What was it he had yelled at her? *Looking good, baaaby!* No doubt he had meant both it and his horn blasting as a compliment, and she should feel flattered. Instead, Cat equated him with the construction workers on the sidewalks of New York, whistling and hollering down from steel beams at unsuspecting women— or looking up their skirts from vantage points below ground level, where bulldozers had gouged deep pits in the earth. "I'll tell you this, Dad—I don't care if they *are* California *boys,* east, west, north or south, men are all alike!"

Still fuming, Cat got into the Jeep and started the engine. Her ankle was swelling up and hurting like the dickens, and at this point all she wanted to do was go home, where she could soak it in some warm salt water. But she did not yet feel confident enough of her driving ability to attempt to turn the vehicle around on the narrow dirt road and so was forced to continue north, searching for someplace where she could maneuver the Jeep about more easily.

It was not long, however, before she spied the Bronco and its infuriating driver ahead of her, no longer going like a bat out of hell, but poking along at a snail's pace. Through the Bronco's rear window, she could see that the driver was now yakking on a cellular telephone. At the sight, some devil seized Cat, and she hit the button that rolled down the window of the front passenger seat of the Jeep. Then, disregarding her injured ankle, she stamped on the accelerator and jammed her hand down on the horn as she whipped into the empty, oncoming lane to pull up alongside the Bronco.

"Hey, you! Eat dirt, you—you...*sodbuster!*" she shouted, to her satisfaction wiping the smug grin off the driver's face before she put the pedal to the metal and raced on by.

Unfortunately for Cat, however, she knew nothing about handling a vehicle while speeding down a dusty country road, and within moments she was fishtailing all over the place, wheels sliding on the sandy dirt. To her horror, the next thing she knew the Jeep was plunging wildly off the road into the shallow ditch and slamming into the trunk of a lone tree that, at the impact, rained chartreuse, grapefruit-size fruit on the vehicle's hood, denting it.

For a moment Cat just sat there dumbly, stunned, shaking, her heart pounding, her one clear thought a silent thanks to God that she had had her seat belt fastened and hadn't gone through the windshield. She was not hurt, she realized at last as she slowly gathered her wits and composure. Just badly rattled, a condition that increased alarmingly when in her rearview mirror she observed the Bronco rolling somehow ominously to a stop behind her. Its engine had barely died before the driver's door was shoved open, and what got out was six feet, two inches of lean, powerful muscle topped by the most ruggedly handsome face she had ever seen and that at the moment had murderous rage written all over it.

Cat was not normally a coward. But as her stricken glance took in not only the figure now stalking her determinedly, but also her isolated surroundings, she thought she would rather be facing a mugger on New York's 42nd Street than the fast-approaching man who looked like some lethal gunslinger stepped from the pages of a Western novel. As they clenched the steering wheel, her hands trembled from both apprehension and guilt. No matter if the brazen man *had* hooted and honked at her, she knew she had no one but herself and her fiery redhead's temper to blame for her current predicament. It was a wonder she had not accidentally run the Bronco off the road, too—a thought she felt certain was uppermost in the man's mind as, in a few long strides, he reached her and wrenched open her door.

"What in the Sam Hill blazes kind of a fool stunt did you think you were pulling, lady?" Morgan bellowed as he stared down furiously at the woman inside the Jeep, his adrenaline pumping, his emotions in such a turmoil that he abruptly did not know which he wanted to do worse: thrash her or kiss her! For the sight of her up close and personal unexpectedly hit him as hard as the chair he had had smashed over his head the last time he had got into a Saturday-night brawl at one of the rowdy local bars, and he felt no less staggered.

God, what a knockout! The woman's long red hair wa tumbled in wild disarray about her pale, piquant face, and her flashing eyes, slanting up at him from beneath her thick, sooty lashes, were so green and brilliant that they momentarily took Morgan's breath away. *Cat eyes...* *bedroom eyes* were the phrases that came unbidden to his mind, made somehow even angrier by his primal-male reaction to her, as he glared down at her. But then a man would have had to be pushing up daisies not to be aroused by those eyes, that mouth—and Morgan was not only alive and kicking, but also in his prime. Sweet heaven, he thought as his gaze was irresistibly drawn to that tempting mouth: moist, wine red, slightly parted, sinfully kissable; the upper lip short, cupid's bow-shaped; the lower lip full, sensuous, sultry. Nor was he oblivious of the tantalizing glimpse of the swell of the woman's ripe, generous breasts, of their shallow rise and fall beneath the wide, scooped neckline of the green knit shell she wore.

"Look, I'm—I'm terribly sorry.... All right?" Instead of appeasing Morgan, however, Cat's low, smoky, faintly breathless voice was like a teasing caress running down his spine. "I—I know you've got every right to be mad—"

"Mad!" Morgan laughed shortly, jeeringly. "Lady, that doesn't even *begin* to describe what I'm feeling right now! Why, I could—" *Snatch you up, fling you down, tear your clothes off and make you beg and moan for mercy* were the words that sprang without warning to his tongue and that, stunned by the wild, primitive notion, he bit back with difficulty. "Horsewhip you," he finished lamely, swallowing hard. "Of all the reckless, foolhardy—"

"I'm—I'm not used to driving, you see," Cat managed to say, still breathless, as though the Jeep's impact had knocked the wind from her—although honesty forced her to admit the sensation was due to the man towering over her.

Although not so heavy, he was as big and tall as her father had been and appeared to be cut from the same rough cloth. His wind-tousled, mahogany brown hair was thick and had a tendency to curl at the collar, and she had a crazy impulse to run her fingers through it, to see if it was as soft and silky as it looked. Framed by equally thick, unruly brows, his eyes gleamed a startling shade of sky blue against his face, which was tanned and weathered from years of exposure to the sun. Beneath his chiseled Roman nose, his sensual mouth was half-hidden by a mustache, against which the whiteness of his even teeth contrasted sharply and which made Cat wonder wildly, inexplicably, if his kisses would tickle her lips.

The short sleeves of his blue chambray work shirt revealed sun-darkened arms corded with muscle, and its open collar exposed a hint of the fine hair that matted his broad chest, which looked somehow as though it ought to have a marshal's badge pinned on it. Encircling his waist was a leather belt with a decorative gold-and-silver buckle engraved with a bronco rider. A pair of jeans clung to his narrow hips and strong thighs. But the gold-nugget-banded Rolex watch he sported on his left wrist, the heavy gold, diamond ring that flashed on his right hand and the ostrich-leather Tony Lama boots he wore informed Cat that while he might look like he'd just ridden in off some high, lonesome trail, he was no ordinary cowboy.

Robert Redford had nothing but a few decades on Morgan McCain.

Breaking the taut, electric silence that had fallen between them, Morgan at last asked gruffly, "Are you hurt?" He felt suddenly ashamed he had not inquired before now, that his temper, as well as his unexpected reaction to the woman, had caused him to rail at her instead—even if she *had* deserved it!

"No," Cat answered, although her hands still shook as, finally recognizing that she ought to get out to investigate the damage to the Jeep, she began to fumble at the clasp on the unfamiliar seat belt, trying to release it.

After a moment, cursing under his breath at her difficulty, Morgan bent, reached inside the Jeep and snapped the clasp open, freeing her. It was an act he had initially hesitated to perform, all too aware of Cat's potent effect upon him. The accidental contact of his strong hand against her slender hip jolted him. He swore softly once more. What in the hell was the matter with him? He felt as though he were a teenager again, his hormones raging clean out of control. The fragrance of Cat's perfume permeated the vehicle, wafted delicately from her skin... White Shoulders, one of Morgan's favorites. His nostrils flared slightly as he inhaled it, thought suddenly of pressing his mouth to the tiny pulse beating rapidly at the hollow of her graceful white throat. As though she were cognizant of his thought, her eyes widened, her lips parted, her breath came in quick little gasps that unintentionally excited him.

Somehow, the interior of the vehicle seemed to Cat both to shrink in size and to rise twenty degrees in temperature in that moment. With Morgan stretched across her, she was vividly conscious of the warmth of his body, of the strength of his arms, of the masculine scents of soap and cologne and sweat that clung to him, of his mouth so tantalizingly close to her own. The inadvertent touch of his hand against her hip was like a shock from a cattle prod, sending a tremor coursing through her and setting her pulse racing. When his narrowed blue eyes pierced her wide-open green ones, she saw in their depths a smoldering desire he did not bother to conceal. At the sight, her gaze fell in embarrassment and confusion and a blush rose to her cheeks. God, she had not felt like this since high school. It really was terribly unnerving, Cat thought, as though a decade of her life had suddenly vanished, taking with it all the confidence and competency she had worked so hard to acquire in the cutthroat, corporate world of New York.

The man was only a rough-diamond cowboy, for heaven's sake! And she was not only on unfamiliar territory, but also grieving, and so in a particularly vulnerable state—and not just mentally, either. She had not seen a house or even another car, except for the Bronco, for miles. She was totally alone with a strange man much bigger and stronger than she, whose eyes said he wanted her. What woman *wouldn't* be unnerved under the circumstances?

As though reading her mind, Morgan declared, "Lucky for you, lady, that I'm not the kind of man to take advantage of a situation like this," as he released her, then assisted her from the Jeep. Cat's knees trembled, and she would have fallen had he not caught her as her injured ankle abruptly gave way beneath her, causing her to stumble against him. "You *are* hurt!" Morgan exclaimed, his concern overriding the sudden tightening in his groin at the feel of the unknown woman in his arms.

"No...yes...well, what I mean is...earlier, when you honked at me, I was startled, and I fell and twisted my ankle," Cat explained, scowling now at the memory and attempting to disengage herself from his grasp, still not trusting him—or herself, either, given how her heart was thudding at his proximity. But Morgan held her fast.

"So that's what got you all riled up, was it?" His eyes now danced unmistakably with mischief, and the lopsided grin he gave her was tinged with wicked insolence. "I tell you what . . . man compliments a pretty woman these days, and instead of thanking him, she labels him a pervert and reaches for her pepper spray! But then I guess I should have known that you'd have a temper to match that fiery red hair of yours! What was it you called me right before you damned near ran me off the road? Sodbuster, wasn't it? Hell. I thought that term went out long before designer jeans, but then I reckon I must have been mistaken on both counts."

His eyes roamed not only with heat, but also with amusement over her Calvin Klein jeans. *Why, he was laughing at her!* No doubt at any moment he would be asking her what was between her and her Calvins. After his previous antics, she wouldn't put it past him!

"Yes, well, I saw that particular epithet used in a Western novel, and it seemed apropos at the time." Cat's tone was tart, intended to put him in his place. "However, I don't believe my temper could possibly be any worse than yours. So why don't we just agree there was provocation on both sides that led to this incident, and let it go at that? Now if you don't mind, I really do need to inspect the damage to the Jeep. It's getting late, and I don't know how long it will take to get a tow truck out here if I have to call one."

Although Morgan released her, he kept a supportive hand beneath her elbow to hold her steady as Cat limped to the front of the vehicle. To her relief, she saw that except for a couple of dents in the hood from the chartreuse, grapefruit-size fruit that now lay scattered on the ground, a mangled bumper and a smashed fog light appeared to be the only real injuries. She had probably done more harm to the old, hard, thorny tree than it had to her.

"Well, the damage isn't too bad. Your Jeep's drivable, at any rate," Morgan announced, confirming her thoughts. "It just needs to be hauled out of the ditch, and I can do that with my Bronco. I'll get my tow chain." Leaving her leaning against the side of the Jeep, he turned away, heading toward his own vehicle.

"Thanks, but I don't want to impose—" Cat began.

"I owe you one. So consider it my way of making up for your sprained ankle," he called back over his shoulder, his mouth curving once more in that impudent, crooked grin of his. It did something strange to her insides.

Once Morgan had maneuvered the Bronco into place and had got out a heavy chain to hitch the two vehicles together, Cat inquired, "What kind of a tree is that?" Its green leaves shone glossily, almost as though they had been waxed. Its trunk, where the bark had been scraped during the accident, revealed an orange core, and its fallen fruit— some of which had broken open to display pulpy, pale yellow insides—had a pungent, distinctive aroma.

"You're not from around these parts, are you?" Morgan glanced up from where he now knelt behind the Jeep, fastening the chain around the axle beneath the cargo space.

"No, I'm—I'm...here on vacation," Cat lied, not wanting to talk about her father's death.

"It's an osage orange...a hedge apple, most people hereabouts call it. Farmers plant 'em for windbreaks usually, although they grow wild, too. Horses generally like the fruit—although I wouldn't recommend your eating it, if that's what you're contemplating."

"No, I was just curious, that's all. I've never had a run-in with a tree before, so I just wanted to know what kind of a tree it was. My mother always used to say that if you *had* to be run over by a car, you should at least pick a Rolls-Royce."

"Well, I'm afraid your choice of tree wasn't quite in that league. A lot of farmers will let you have dead hedge free for firewood if you just come clear it off their land. Hedge burns real hot and shoots sparks all over the place." Morgan's eyes glinted as he looked up at her intently.

If there were, as it seemed, a double entendre to his words, Cat chose to ignore it—just as she determinedly attempted to ignore the heat and sparks that continued to flare between her and Morgan, as though electricity crackled and arced tangibly between them. She averted her gaze, flushing again, and with a sigh and a shrug, Morgan returned to his task.

"Do you need me to get back into the Jeep, to put the gearshift into Neutral or something?" Cat asked once he had finished coupling the two vehicles together.

"Yes, I do." Minutes later Morgan had the Jeep hauled from the ditch and unhooked from the Bronco. Coiling up the heavy chain he had used, he approached the driver's side of the Jeep, where Cat now sat inside the vehicle, its engine running. He hesitated for a moment over the words that sprang to his mind. Then he thought, *What the hell...no drill, no well,* and he spoke. "Look, I know we've only just met and all, and that we sort of got off on the wrong foot, besides. But, well, how 'bout if I buy you supper tonight to make up for today?"

To say she was not tempted by his offer would have been a lie, Cat knew. But she had never in her life succumbed to a one-night stand, even with a man who was *not* a stranger to her, and she was not about to start now. Although she suspected Morgan was truly nothing more than what she had in the past heard her father refer to as a "good ole boy," her life in New York had made her naturally wary and distrustful. Still, she smiled to take the sting from her response.

"Thank you," she said pointedly, remembering his earlier remark about compliments, perverts and pepper spray. "I'm flattered...really, I am. And I *do* appreciate your time and trouble in helping me get the Jeep back on the road. But—"

"But your mother warned you never to speak to strangers and never, ever to go off someplace alone with a strange man," Morgan finished wryly.

"Yes, something like that." Cat nodded.

"Well, you can't blame a guy for trying." A *tsk* of regret issuing from one corner of his mouth, Morgan shook his head ruefully, making light of his disappointment. "Still, for all its city status, Wichita's basically a small town at heart, so maybe I'll see you around, huh?"

"Maybe," Cat agreed, glad and relieved he had not turned ugly and made some cocky, insulting remark about her not knowing what she was missing, as though he were the biggest stud around and she were a frigid fool. "You just never know. If there's one thing I've learned in life, it's to expect the unexpected."

"More words of wisdom from your mother?" Morgan lifted one brow teasingly.

"No... from my—from my father." Cat's voice caught at the memory, and as she felt tears fill her eyes afresh, she said quickly, "Well, thanks again for all your help." Then she put the automatic gearshift into Drive and hurriedly pulled away, leaving Morgan standing there gazing after her thoughtfully, feeling a peculiar, inexplicable sense of loss and cursing himself soundly when he realized abruptly that he had not even learned her name.

Four

A Case of Mistaken Identities

Although it certainly was not out of the ordinary for Morgan to dine alone, he seemed somehow tonight to feel the solitude worse than usual. The prime rib he ordered at the upscale Chelsea Bar & Grill was excellent, as always, yet despite his hunger, he found he could not concentrate on his meal. As he gazed at the talking, laughing couples gathered around the piano bar, his mind kept dwelling on how different the evening would have been had the unknown redhead with the fiery temper agreed to join him. She had possessed a sass and spunk that had intrigued him—not to mention a gorgeous face and body that had cried out to him like a sweetly deceptive siren's. She had been ... special, somehow. And he had not had sense enough to find out her name or even to write down her license-tag number so he could track her down later by means of his considerable computer resources.

Damn! Was he slipping or what? A few months ago he would have charmed that redhead not only into having supper with him, but also into his bed afterward. Why had he not pressed her harder? Was it because he had finally and truly tired of that game? Was it because now, at Frank's death, he, Morgan, had begun to feel his own mortality more keenly, to recognize and to admit to himself at long last that he *did* want more out of life than just the footloose and fancy-free bachelor's existence he led? A home instead of a town house. A wife instead of a string of affairs and one-night stands. A couple of kids instead of an aquarium full of fish. Was it because he had begun to question what all he had worked so hard to achieve was for, if not for that? Damn it! He did not want to wind up like Frank—alone and dead of a heart attack before he was even sixty. What was it his partner had always said? *Life's a bitch, and then you die, Son.* No, there had to be more to life than that—or what was the point?

Following supper, Morgan returned home to his town house in The Mews, waving perfunctorily at the guard, who admitted him through the gate of the enclave clustered on the western edge of Vickridge. Once inside, Morgan tossed his key ring on the kitchen counter and grabbed a beer from the refrigerator. From the freezer he withdrew a package of frozen brine shrimp, a portion of which he cut into chunks and fed to the fish in his aquarium. Then he checked his answering machine. The red light was blinking, indicating a message had been received in his absence. He punched the Rewind button and, while the tape was running back to its starting position, twisted the cap off the bottled beer and took a long swallow. When the tape had come to a stop, he pressed the Play button.

"Morgan, this is Virginia Lorimer," a woman's plaintive voice announced from the machine. "I hesitated calling you, because I really do hate to bother you, especially at such a sorrowful time as this and so soon after poor

Frank's funeral—such a nice service you had for him, by
the way! I'm sure he would have been so proud of it! And
I guess I probably ought to have called the police instead.... But, well, I just didn't want to cause any unnec-
essary trouble for you, you understand, if it was only you
going through Frank's business papers and personal belongings, sorting them out and all...."

"Yeah, so get to the point already, why don't you, Virginia?" Morgan muttered as he took another sip of beer
and listened impatiently to Frank's nosy, half-crocked
neighbor.

"But if it wasn't you over at Frank's yesterday evening," Viriginia's voice droned on, "then I really think someone's broken into his house, and that you should go over
right away and investigate, because I saw lights on there last
night. I know I did! And I've heard there are some rob-
bers, you know—as unconscionable as it certainly is—who
actually read the obituary columns in the newspapers,
looking for easy marks... houses that are standing empty
due to their owners' deaths. And of course, Frank's address being what it is, that house of his must surely be a
temptation to thieves.... Oh, I'm probably just a nervous
old Nellie, and it was only you at Frank's house. But, well,
you can't be too careful these days, and so I thought you
should know, that's all. Again, I'm sorry to have dis-
turbed you, Morgan." There was a short click as Viriginia
rang off. Then, with a brief hiss, the tape wound to a stop.

"Wonder if you saw the lights at Frank's house before or
after you'd started hitting the sauce for the evening,
Virginia?" Morgan mused dryly, shaking his head and
rolling his eyes, knowing it was a wonder the woman had
not called the police—and reported that lights were
streaming from a UFO that had landed in Frank's backyard!

Poor Virginia! Well, that was what came of having too
much money to spend, too much time on your hands and

too little excitement in your life. You wound up as the neighborhood's resident moralist, snoop and crackpot—taking pictures of your neighbors' houses to prove to your homeowners' association that the Smiths lacked the requisite number of trees in their yard or that the Joneses were concealing a forbidden satellite dish in their bushes!

God, Morgan thought as he groaned inwardly, *spare me from the Virginia Lorimers of this world!* Still, no matter what he thought of her, he supposed he would have to go by Frank's house later to check it out and make certain it really *hadn't* been broken into—simply because there was always the slim possibility that this time Virginia was not just crying wolf. Nevertheless, Morgan intended to finish his beer first—and maybe even have a second one—and read his mail and watch the 10:00 p.m. news, as well. Then, even though he felt sure Virginia's suspicion was entirely ungrounded, he would, on his nightly jog through the neighborhood, cruise by Frank's house.

Now that she was no longer jet lagged and exhausted, Cat realized for the first time how big and empty and lonely her father's house was. It might as well have been standing all by itself out in the country, such was the silence that enveloped it. Accustomed to the hustle and bustle of New York, to the sounds of the neighbors in her apartment building, of the incessant traffic and subway trains, of the night life in a city that never slept, she found the lack of noise disturbing. It was as though, somehow, she were all alone in the world—an eerie, unsettling sensation.

To dispel it and fill up the silence, Cat turned on the small television that sat on the kitchen counter as she limped around her father's country kitchen, fixing herself a simple dinner consisting of a tossed salad and a chicken potpie. While the potpie was baking, she soaked her ankle in a stainless-steel mixing bowl filled with warm salt water, which so helped the swelling and eased the pain that she knew her sprain was not serious, just a nuisance. Afterward she ate at the kitchen table, in front of the television.

Other than the news, Cat didn't watch much television usually. But her father's house was hooked up to cable, and so, a little to her surprise, she discovered myriad channels from which to choose. With the remote control she flicked through them one by one until her eye was caught by an old movie, *Butch Cassidy and the Sundance Kid,* starring Paul Newman and Robert Redford. All at once Cat was struck by the resemblance between Redford and the cowboy who had so infuriated and attracted her earlier that day. The unknown man had been a younger, darker version of the actor, she realized now. Thousands of women would, given the opportunity, run off with Redford, she knew. Was it any wonder she should have felt her pulse quicken in the presence of the actor's look-alike?

Now, however, Cat felt horribly guilty that the cowboy had managed, even for so short a while, to force her thoughts away from her father's death. It was not unusual to be drawn to another human being sexually in the face of death, to be driven by a primal urge to create life; and her father would not have condemned her for that. Still, she chastised herself for having a hard time putting the unknown man from her mind.

Cat watched the entire movie, sobbing more than she normally would have at its end, grieving for her father and wondering for the first time if she had perhaps been too hasty in breaking off her engagement to Spence. It was not a crime to be single, and it was certainly possible to live a full, happy life without ever having married. But despite her professional career and independence, her heart cried out for companionship and children. As greedy as it might seem, she wanted all life had to offer.

Having finished her meal, Cat rinsed her few dishes and stacked them in the dishwasher. Then, feeling terribly depressed, she went upstairs to get ready for bed. A long hot bath was in order, she decided, followed by immersion in the pages of some favorite novel, or she would not sleep well tonight. She flicked on the lights and the television in her bedroom, setting the channel to CNN. For a moment she yearned desperately to telephone Spence. But the memory of their argument and breakup, of his firing her so callously, followed so hard on the heels by her father's death, dissuaded her from weakening and giving in to the temptation. She was made of sterner and more prideful stuff than to go crawling back to Spence, who had wanted just another showy possession instead of a wife.

Once more, thoughts of the cowboy intruded in Cat's mind. He had been vibrant and earthy, the kind of man, she had sensed, to fling a woman down upon the ground, taking her in the tumultuous heat of passion—a notion from which fastidious Spence would have shrunk, labeling it common and uncivilized. But somehow Cat could not put from her head the idea that a woman lying beneath that unknown man would feel not only the earth, but also the heavens move for her, that he would make damned sure she felt it!

Smiling despite herself at the thought, she settled into the warm water of the sunken, marble bathtub, leaning back, closing her eyes and letting the scented bubbles engulf her.

Hell's bells! For once in her life, Virginia Lorimer had *not* been pulling a Chicken Little, Morgan thought, stunned, as he stared at the lights glowing softly from behind the closed plantation shutters that screened the casement windows of Frank's house. Somebody had indeed broken into the place, might even at this moment still be ransacking it! At the thought, Morgan felt hot rage boil up inside him, as though it were his town house that had been violated. His parents had been killed in a car accident when he was a youth. An elderly, widowed great-aunt had taken him in and reared him until he was old enough to be out on his own. So, for all practical purposes, Frank Devlin had been the only father he had known for most his life. Morgan's eyes narrowed murderously. Come hell or high water, he was going to get the bastard who had dared to break into Frank's house!

As Morgan advanced stealthily up the driveway, he realized there was no unfamiliar vehicle parked out front, half loaded with the burglar's loot. But then it was not uncommon, he knew, for a thief to steal a victim's own car during a robbery, using it to carry away the illicit haul. Frank had owned both a Jeep and a classic Cadillac convertible. Jeeps were popular at chop shops, and the Cadillac was worth a mint; either one would bring a tidy, however illegal, profit.

The front door appeared secure, as did the front windows. So Morgan crept around the side of the house and vaulted over the high wooden fence into the backyard. As he did, from Virginia Lorimer's house next door, the furious, high-pitched yapping of her two cockapoos reached his ears. Minutes later her exterior security lights blazed on, her back door opened, she herself poked her head out and the two little dogs came barking and bounding out into her backyard, to race alongside the fence between her property and Frank's.

"Damn it, Virginia!" Morgan yelled to her above the ruckus. "It's me, Morgan. Call those mutts of yours back inside!"

"Oh, my goodness gracious!" Virginia laid one hand against her breast, visibly agitated. "What a fright you gave me, Morgan! My heart's just pounding! Why, I'll be lucky if I don't follow poor Frank to the grave! Muffin! Crumpet! Come here, darlings. It's only Morgan McCain. You know Morgan, babies...poor Frank's partner. What're you doing out there in the dark, Morgan, prowling around like some Peeping Tom? Is everything all right?"

"Yes," he lied, wanting to be rid of her as quickly as possible. "Everything's fine. I've been out jogging, and I just dropped by to check on Frank's house, that's all. Now, for heaven's sake, go back inside before those mutts of yours wake up the entire neighborhood!" he hissed angrily, glancing anxiously at Frank's place, wondering if all the noise had alerted whoever was inside. "Good *night,* Virginia!" he said firmly when she continued to peer at him curiously from her doorway.

"Well, if you're sure nothing's wrong... Good night, Morgan."

Finally, to his relief, she withdrew, taking the two cockapoos with her. Her security lights winked out shortly afterward—although he spied her at a window, furtively drawing back her drapes to peek out at him. He cursed and groaned inwardly, wondering how Frank had not only endured her, but had actually taken her out more than once. Then Morgan chided himself for his irritability. Virginia was a widow, and lonely. She was probably feeling Frank's loss as keenly as Morgan himself was. Still, right now he would gladly have pitched those two mutts of hers into the Big Arkansas river!

Forcing himself to tamp down his anger, he carefully skirted the swimming pool and hot tub, then sneaked across the multilevel wooden deck to the French doors at the back of Frank's house, which were also secure. To gain entry, the thief must have broken a side window somewhere or somehow gained access through the garage, Morgan thought. Withdrawing from the inside pocket of his sweatpants his set of keys to Frank's house, Morgan inserted the proper one into the lock of the French doors and turned it. Moments later he stood inside the house, warily surveying his surroundings and certain now from the noises he heard coming from upstairs that he was not alone.

* * *

It was the dogs' feverish yapping that attracted Cat's attention as she stepped from the bathtub and began to towel herself dry. Since, earlier, the neighborhood had been so quiet, she was intelligent enough to realize something must have stirred the dogs up, and because she was alone, she was prudent enough to investigate the cause. Slipping into her panties and a vibrant, lime green caftan, she limped to her father's dark bedroom at the back of the house, where she peered through the open wooden slats of the plantation shutters that screened the casement windows. The barking of the dogs, which had seemed to be coming from beyond the backyard, had now ceased. But as she peeked out, Cat observed in the moonlight the shadowy figure of a man on the lawn, moving furtively toward the French doors.

Her mouth went dry and her heart pounded with fear as she tried to remember whether she had set the alarm before coming upstairs. She was almost positive she had not, so there was no use in counting on its going off to summon assistance. She was on her own. Even as she watched, the man disappeared from her view. Moments later, before she could even think what to do, Cat heard one of the French doors open and realized he must have jimmied the lock, was even now inside the house with her! God, the irony of it! In all the years she had lived in New York, she had never even been mugged. The idea that she was now perhaps about to be robbed, raped and murdered in Wichita, Kansas, in the very center of America's Heartland, was so ludicrous that she nearly laughed aloud with hysteria.

Torn, panicked, Cat glanced longingly at the telephone on her father's nightstand. Aid was surely only a phone call away. But then she thought that even if the 911 emergency number was not busy, there was no telling how long it would take for the police to arrive; and every passing minute of delay might prove fatal. No, she had to get out, to get away! Even if none of the neighbors would help her, there had been a guard posted at The Mews, the enclave of town houses clustered at the western edge of Vickridge. Physically, Cat was in excellent shape from her three-times-weekly workouts at a gym. Even barefoot and with a sprained ankle, she could run as far as the guard tower if she had to, she decided resolutely. Slowly, she crept from her father's bedroom and started down the back staircase that led to the kitchen, praying that whoever was in the house would hear the noise of her television upstairs and would move in that direction, toward the front staircase, hoping to take her by surprise.

As she reached the foot of the stairs, Cat paused for a surreptitious look around the corner of the wall. To her terror, she spied the intruder standing in the family room beyond the big, open country kitchen. She clapped one hand to her mouth to stifle the gasp of shock and fright that rose in her throat. It was *him!* The cowboy who had hollered and honked at her earlier, who had towed the Jeep from the ditch and then asked her to dinner. Oh, God, her initial assumption about him must have been correct! He was some kind of a lunatic, a pervert—a *stalker!* Doubtless enraged by her refusal of his invitation, he had followed her home and had broken into the house, intending heaven only knew what. Oh, God, he was leaving the family room and coming into the kitchen, moving toward *her!* Some sound must have passed her lips after all, alerting him to her presence....

If she ran back upstairs, she might be trapped up there, unable to escape from the house, Cat realized, the wheels of her brain churning furiously. Quickly, she dropped down to her hands and knees so the kitchen counters and cabinets would, she prayed, hide her from the man's view as she skittered across the kitchen floor into the dining room. Just inside the doorway a huge vase sat upon the massive sideboard against the wall. With trembling hands Cat snatched up the vase, her heart in her throat as she heard the man's footsteps drawing ominously nearer. Evidently, he must have seen or heard her and was now coming toward the dining room. When he entered, she did not hesitate, but smashed the vase down as hard as she could upon his head.

She heard the man groan and then, with a loud thud, hit the floor as the vase shattered about him. Hurriedly, Cat reached out and switched on the dining room light, gasping again at the sight that met her eyes. The man was knocked out cold, sprawled half on, half off the Oriental carpet laid upon the hardwood floor, shards of the broken vase scattered all around him. For a moment, as she stared at her handiwork, Cat could only think dumbly that she had probably just destroyed a priceless Ming vase. Then she remembered that her father would not have known the Ming Dynasty from Ming of Mongo, and relief that owed a great deal more to her own survival than to the vase's maker flooded her being.

Gingerly stepping over sharp pieces of china, she hastened to the kitchen and picked up the receiver of the telephone, her hands shaking as she dialed 911. Thank God she didn't get a busy signal, that the phone actually rang! Within moments Cat was assured by the dispatcher that the police were en route, and much to her surprise and relief, they actually did arrive approximately ten minutes later, along with paramedics. She admitted them all to the house, explaining the situation to one of the two police officers, while the two paramedics treated the injuries the intruder had sustained from the blow of the heavy vase: minor cuts and bruises and a possible concussion.

After several minutes the second police officer, who had checked the interior pocket of the intruder's sweatpants for identification and then, finding none, had examined the house, returned to the scene in the dining room. His face was puzzled and suspicious now when he looked at her, Cat thought in confusion as he drew his fellow officer aside.

They spoke in low tones before turning their attention back to her.

"Ma'am," one of them began, "we seem to have a slight problem here concerning your story. You see, we can't find any signs of the forced entry you described—"

"That's because I let myself in with a damned key!" Morgan interjected surlily as he impatiently waved away the paramedics and hauled himself up into one of the high-backed chairs around the dining table, from where he glared groggily at Cat.

"A *key!*" she cried, stunned by his audacity, his brazen lying to the police. "How could you possibly have a key to my father's house?"

"Your *father!* Damn, damn, *damn!* I knew it! The minute I came to and saw you here, I just *knew* it!" Morgan groaned, shaking his head disbelievingly as he gingerly probed the huge, swollen knot just above his right ear. "Coldcocked by a woman, by God!" he exclaimed sourly. "I'll never live it down." Then he held out his hands to the startled, bemused police officers, as though expecting, indeed *wanting,* to be cuffed and hauled away to jail. "Just clap 'em on and take me in, boys," he drawled mockingly. "I want to wake up in a jail cell tomorrow morning and find out this has all been just another Saturday night in Margaritaville, the product of an imagination unhinged by booze.... Will you *please* get that penlight out of my eyes!" he snapped to the paramedics, who, thinking he was rambling and confused, unaware of the seriousness of his situation, were attempting to recheck the dilation and contraction of his pupils. "I've got a hard head, I've been hit harder in the past and there's nothing wrong with me that a couple of aspirin won't cure!" Morgan paused for a moment, then addressed Cat again. "Ms. Devlin...you *are* Ms. Catherine Devlin, are you not?"

"Yes, but how did *you* know that?" she asked, a strange, sinking feeling of suspicion and mortification suddenly taking hold of her.

"I know...I know because I am your father's friend and business partner, Ms. Devlin...Morgan McCain," he announced. Stunned, Cat could only stare at him speechlessly as, in the abrupt silence, the front doorbell rang, accompanied by the high-pitched yapping of dogs, and he continued ruefully, "And *that* will be Virginia Lorimer, your nosy next-door neighbor—and the cause of this entire damned mess!"

Five

Getting to Know You

Chuckling with a good deal of amusement, the police and paramedics had left. Apologizing plaintively and defending herself profusely all the while, Virginia Lorimer had finally departed as well, taking away with her the two barking cockapoos, much to Cat's and Morgan's mutual relief. Now they sat alone in the taut, strained silence that had descended in her father's family room, to which they had retired, staring at each other with a mixture of wariness and ruefulness and, still, a measure of disbelief.

Cat could not seem to take in the fact that this man, this cowboy, was her father's friend and business partner, Morgan McCain. In the past, whenever she had thought of Morgan at all, she had, from her father's wild stories and descriptions of him, vaguely envisioned a banty, beer-swilling braggart and brawler who mistakenly believed himself to be God's gift to women, not this tall, rugged, drop-dead-gorgeous man who sat in the chair next to her own, his cool, commanding presence such that he seemed effortlessly to dominate his surroundings.

Morgan was equally slow to absorb the fact that this woman was Frank Devlin's daughter, Catherine...*Cat,* she called herself. He ought to have recognized Frank's Jeep earlier today, he thought dumbly as he gazed at her, feeling like a poleaxed steer and wondering if perhaps he had been too hasty, after all, in refusing to permit the paramedics to take him to the hospital, in case her crack upon his skull had indeed given him a concussion. Then he realized that, of course, there were hundreds of Jeeps in town and that there had been no reason at the time to connect with Frank the one that she had been driving. In fact, Morgan mused, it was just as well he had *not* made the connection, because then his first meeting with her would surely have gone a whole lot differently. His temper would undoubtedly have led him to say things to her he would be deeply regretting at this moment. Awkwardly, Morgan cleared his throat.

"Somehow, we...ah...seem to keep getting off on the wrong foot, don't we?" he observed at last, thinking uncomfortably that Cat was nothing at all as he had imagined her. He had expected someone hard, aloof, sophisticated...cold—not this beautiful, graceful young woman whose dark red hair seemed afire and whose porcelain skin radiated such warmth in the lamplight. Whose green eyes could dance with humor, flash sparks of indignation and harbor shadows of deep anguish all at once when they met his glance. "Why didn't you let me know you were coming to Wichita? I would have been more than happy to pick you up at the airport, to see that you were settled in and had everything you needed."

"Thank you for the thought. But I...needed some time alone...to think, to grieve," Cat responded quietly. "Dad's death was so unexpected, so painful—" She broke off abruptly, tears filling her eyes. Glancing away from him, she bit her lower lip hard, so plainly embarrassed by her uncontrollable display of emotion that Morgan knew it was unfeigned, that despite his previous doubts to the contrary, Ms. Catherine Devlin had, in fact, loved her father wholeheartedly. For a few minutes she fought for composure, finally regaining it. Then she continued. "As you can see, it . . . hit me pretty hard. I still can't quite believe he's gone. Somehow I keep expecting to hear his voice, his laughter—"

"Yeah, I know what you mean," Morgan admitted, his own voice gruff with emotion.

Cat started a little at his tone, for the first time realizing she was not alone in her sorrow, that Morgan had cared about Frank Devlin, too.

"I'm sorry," she said, after a long moment spent contemplating that fact. "I didn't think about Dad being your business partner, your friend. His death must have been difficult for you, too. . . . And I haven't even thanked you for—for taking care of him, for making all the funeral arrangements and everything for me when I couldn't get back here from Europe in time."

"Frank was like a father to me. I was glad to do it."

Something about the way Morgan spoke those simple words made Cat understand their truth. It struck her suddenly that although her father had never married again, he might have wanted to. He might have longed for a second wife, a second family . . . or at least a son, someone to follow in his footsteps, someone to value, hold on to and to build upon all he had worked so hard to achieve in his life. She had not until this moment ever thought of herself as that person, although she had loved her father dearly. Perhaps, she reflected now, surprised and curious and even faintly piqued, her father, despite his own love for her, had not thought of her in that light, either. Perhaps, as he had been like a father to Morgan, Morgan had been to him the

son he had never had, the heir apparent, the one to whom
the proverbial torch could be safely passed on.

Involuntarily, Cat felt her eyes being drawn to Morgan's
hands. They were strong, sure, capable hands, she knew
instinctively, callused and accustomed to hard work, despite the fact that they were well shaped and well groomed,
with a light dusting of dark hair upon their backs. They
were hands to be trusted, she thought. She remembered
how they had so easily released her seat belt, had held and
supported her so firmly, had unwittingly made her skin
tingle—and yet had done nothing untoward.

Yes, her father would have trusted those hands; he would
have trusted Morgan McCain.

"Would you—would you like a drink? Or—or some
coffee?" Cat asked abruptly on impulse, cursing her
wretched tongue for stumbling over the words, for making
her feel like a blushing schoolgirl again. In the space of half
a day, this man, this cowboy, had somehow succeeded in
affecting her in ways she had not until now thought possible. She did not know why that should be so; she knew only
that it was. "I could make some coffee…it would only take
a few minutes."

It was late, and Morgan knew he should go. Yet he found
himself curiously loath to leave Cat. Was it only this
morning he had yearned for just ten minutes of her precious time, so he could tell her exactly what he had thought
of her? He wanted to give her something now, but not a
piece of his mind—as his sweatpants would certainly reveal if he got to his feet. Damn! Did she know how she
looked sitting there, curled up in one of the family room's
oversize, stuffed chairs, her hair aflame and one creamy
shoulder bared where the sleeve of her caftan had slipped
a little down her arm? Just looking at her, just thinking
about sweeping her up in his arms, carrying her upstairs
and pressing her down upon that big, antique canopy bed
he knew Frank had bought for her was making Morgan

crazy inside. His groin was tight with desire. He had better go before he made a complete fool of himself again!

"I'd love some coffee," he heard himself answer instead, as though his mouth had without warning disengaged itself from his brain, deliberately and maddeningly hooking up with another portion of his anatomy, a portion notorious for its lack of common sense.

But it was too late now to withdraw his acceptance of Cat's offer. She had already risen from her chair and stepped quickly into the kitchen, as though glad to have something to do. In light of that, he would appear rude and churlish if he left now, Morgan knew. So instead, he joined her in the kitchen, taking a seat at the table, watching her appreciatively as she moved about, grinding aromatic coffee beans for the basket filter in the drip coffeemaker on the counter, adding water, then turning on the machine. From a bag, she took fresh bagels, warming them before arranging them attractively on a platter, along with small bowls of spreadable fruit and low-fat Philadelphia cream cheese. Morgan was not normally much of a bagel eater, thinking of it as an East Coast preference. But he had to admit Cat had somehow made the bagels seem pretty appetizing— even if he was also simultaneously amused by the thought that she might have been laying out a high tea. She might not be the stuck-up, hard-hearted witch he had initially supposed, but he was willing to bet he had been right about one thing: her background and upbringing were such that she would know which fork to use when at a seven-course dinner.

Still, much to his surprise as he watched her preparations, Morgan found it difficult to refrain from imagining Cat belonged to him, that it was his kitchen in which she worked so gracefully and competently, and that after they had drunk their coffee and eaten their bagels, he would have every right to take her upstairs and make love to her. That was only a fantasy, but he suspected something of his thoughts must have shown on his face, because when she joined him at the table, a blush stained her cheeks and she concentrated more than necessary on spreading cream cheese on her bagel.

In fact, Cat was not aware of his thoughts. It was her own that so unsettled her. It had come to her while she worked how at ease Morgan was in her father's house, her father's kitchen, as though he belonged there and she were somehow an interloper. She had felt suddenly out of her milieu and depth, had experienced again that strange sensation she had had in the taxi from the airport—that she had somehow been transported back in time. She had felt as though she were lost somewhere on the wild frontier, with only this cowboy to depend upon for survival. Inexplicably, the image of Robert Redford in the movie she'd just seén kept filling her mind, specifically the scene in which Katherine Ross's character, Etta Place, had been undressing in her bedroom, initially oblivious of the presence of Redford's character, Harry Longbaugh, the Sundance Kid. When Etta had finally spied him, the Kid had drawn his gun and insisted she keep right on taking off her clothes for him—so when Cat had sat down across the table from Morgan, she had been abruptly seized by a crazy notion that he was about to level a revolver at her and demand she undress for him . . . slowly, very slowly. She had been both mortified and perversely excited by the idea, and she had not dared to look at him in that moment, for fear he might somehow discern her thoughts.

Now, as she glanced up at him surreptitiously from beneath the fringe of her lashes, Cat silently cursed the fact that all the polite conversation she could usually and easily indulge in to entertain a guest seemed to have deserted her. And the suggestion of her college-speech-class professor—to conquer stage fright by imagining one's audience as being totally naked—did not produce the desired effect at all when she envisioned Morgan McCain without any clothes on. In fact, as the image of him nude rose in her mind, Cat's heart beat even faster, and she could hardly swallow the bite of bagel she had chewed into mush. What was the matter with her? Why should this man disconcert her so? He was *only* a man, like any other—and as a professional, independent woman who had just broken off her engagement, it would not be wholly amiss of her at the moment to feel nothing but contempt for the entire male gender. Instead, she was sitting here fantasizing about going to bed with Morgan McCain! There was definitely something wrong with her, Cat decided. Grief and jet lag must somehow have combined to derange her brain!

"The coffee's very good," Morgan said, interrupting her reverie and then repeating his comment when Cat momentarily stared at him blankly.

"Oh...the coffee...thanks. I'm glad you like it. It's a special gourmet blend. I bought it at the grocery store earlier today, and since I'm not familiar with Midwestern brands, I wasn't sure how it would taste. But I thought I'd give it a try, anyway." Jeez Louise, she sounded like a babbling idiot unable to make any intelligent conversation whatsoever! He was probably sitting there thinking, *Ditsy redhead!* and wondering how he could politely escape from her. She could not remember the last time she had felt so awkward, so inadequate, and she did not like the feeling now.

Everything's just been too much for you. You're overwhelmed at the moment, Cat, and therefore off-balance, she told herself sternly. *You need to recover your equilibrium, that's all. You can get through this, one day at a time.*

"I'm sorry," she said then. "I don't normally chatter on so inanely. I've been under a lot of stress, as I'm sure you have, too." She paused for a moment. "I'd like to hear about my father...what kind of service you had for him and where he's—where he's buried. And I'm certain there are things you'd like to discuss as well—business matters..."

"Yes, there are. But it *is* late, and it's been a long day besides—a very long, *befuddled* day." Morgan smiled ruefully, thinking of all the bizarre twists and turns that had led them, finally, to be having coffee in Frank's kitchen. "I'm sure you're tired, and I know *I* am. So tell you what— why don't I meet you here in the morning? That way we can get the Jeep in to be repaired so you'll have a car you can depend on...you won't want to drive the Cadillac, I know, since it's so big. Then I'll take you out to the cemetery. After that, we'll grab some lunch, and I'll see if we can't meet with your father's attorney, Richard Hollis, sometime tomorrow afternoon to take care of all the legalities. How does that sound to you?"

"Fine. That sounds just fine," Cat responded, trying to quell the sudden racing of her pulse at the idea of spending the day with Morgan McCain. He was just a man, like any other, nothing special, she insisted again to herself. Still, the glance he gave her as he finished his coffee and then stood made her heart turn over.

"I'll see you in the morning then," he said as she walked him to the front door.

"I'll—I'll...be here." Jeez Louise, she had almost replied, *I'll be looking forward to it,* as though she were some eager puppy wagging its tail at the sight of a dog biscuit! She had better get hold of herself in a hurry, Cat thought. "Good night, Morgan."

"Good night, Cat."

He jogged off into the darkness, and after she closed the front door behind him, she leaned against it weakly for a moment, her knees trembling.

"Cat Devlin, you're a grieving fool on the rebound!" she declared aloud to herself.

But as she started upstairs to bed, her step was lighter than it had been for many days.

Six

Hellos and Goodbyes

When Cat awakened in the morning, it was to the sound of what she initially supposed was the digital alarm clock on the nightstand beside her bed, which she had set before retiring. But after she blearily groped for the clock and pressed its Snooze button, and the ringing continued, she realized finally that it was the telephone echoing so jarringly in her ear. Belatedly fumbling for and then lifting the receiver, she spoke.

"Hello." She was still not quite awake. Her voice was soft, smoky, drowsy.

"You know, you can tell an awful lot about a woman from how she sounds when you roust her out of bed in the morning," a low, husky, baritone voice drawled provocatively. "Now you . . . you sound sleepy—and sexy as hell."

"Who . . . who is this?" she asked, her pulse leaping

suddenly, because she already half suspected her caller's identity, since no one else knew she was in town.

"It's Morgan," he confirmed. "I'll be over in an hour."

Feeling like the world's worst fool, Morgan hung up without giving her a chance to reply. He had not intended to greet her in such a manner; the words had seemed to come from his mouth of their own volition. It was as though, ever since he had met Cat Devlin, he had been possessed by some uncontrollable devil. If he had not rung off, he knew his next line would have been, "And there's nothing I'd like better than to find you still in bed, waiting for me." At the thought, unbidden, the image of Cat lying upstairs in that big canopy bed, half-asleep, wearing a diaphanous negligee that was half slipping from her shoulders rose in his mind, arousing him unbearably. "Get a grip, McCain," he chided himself wryly. "She's just a woman, like any other." But somehow he couldn't seem to make himself believe that.

A cold shower. That was what he needed—a long, cold shower. Groaning at the thought, but resolutely compelling himself to move anyway, Morgan abruptly flung back the sheets and stumbled naked from his bed to his bathroom. He turned on the radio as he passed it, cranking up the volume so he would be able to hear it over the water. Then he opened the shower door, twisted on the Cold tap and forced himself to step inside the tiled enclosure. The sharp, icy spray hit him full blast, effectively quelling his amorous musings. Simultaneously, over the sound of the running water, he made out the opening strains of "What I Did for Love." The irony of that was *not* amusing. Wincing and shivering, he sighed heavily.

It was going to be one of those days.

It's a beautiful day! Cat thought as she scrambled from bed and headed toward her bathroom, flicking on her stereo in passing. The tuner, she had discovered yesterday, was set to a channel called B98-FM, an adult-contemporary station that suited her just fine. As she twisted her dark red hair up on top of her head and, with a French comb, secured the loose ends, she hummed along to the song that was currently playing, "What I Did for Love." The loss of her father still grieved her; she would miss him a lot. But now she felt that, by coming to Wichita, she had somehow encouraged the healing process to begin. It was almost as though, here, her father were still with her in spirit, looking over her shoulder and cheering her on. Involuntarily, she kept thinking of that last line in his letter to her, about her and Morgan being two wildcats, together at last.

"Dad, you old matchmaker, you!" she said ruefully as she turned on the shower and slipped off her negligee. "Why do I have the sneaking suspicion that of all the men you could have picked, this rough-diamond cowboy was the one you thought was right for me, huh? He's nothing at all like Spence—but no doubt you considered that a mark in Morgan's favor, right? Well, we'll see. No matter what you might have thought, the truth is things really haven't gone too smoothly between me and Morgan up until this point— and I'll admit that just for a moment this morning, I was half-afraid he was an obscene caller! He's lucky I didn't hang up on him or, worse yet, blow a whistle in his ear!"

Had Morgan still been lying in bed when he had telephoned her? Cat wondered as the warm spray from the shower head poured over her nude body. And if he had been, what had he been wearing? Pajamas? Boxer shorts? Briefs? Nothing at all?

"What's it to you, Cat? I mean...it's not like you're going to go to bed with the man or anything. Why, you hardly even know him!"

But while there might be some accounting for taste, there was, Cat knew, none at all for chemistry. That was something that just happened. As much as she longed to deny it, and despite the fact that they had twice now got off to a bad start, she knew deep down inside that embers smoldered between her and Morgan, just waiting to be ignited, to explode into something that half frightened and half tantalized her. Still, she was smart enough to realize she was terribly vulnerable right now, not only because of her father's death, but also because of her breakup with Spence. Under the circumstances, a relationship with a man was the last thing she needed to be embarking upon! Her current mental state was assuredly affecting her good judgment.

"Get hold of yourself, Cat!" she told herself sternly as, after stepping from the shower, she toweled herself dry. "Otherwise, you're liable to wind up making a complete fool of yourself! For all you know, Morgan McCain might not want anything more from you than a one-night stand—and your father's shares in the One-Eyed Jacks Oil and Gas Company!"

This last was a sobering thought—one Cat had not previously considered. Of course, Morgan would be concerned about the future of his corporation and its disposition. Abruptly, some of the joy went out of the morning, and it was with a much cooler head and a steadier hand that Cat finished applying her makeup. After that, she dressed in a becoming, peach-colored linen suit and was downstairs, finishing a quick cup of coffee, when Morgan at last rang the doorbell.

When she opened the door, he did a double take at the sight of her, not quite sure for a moment that he was at the right house. There was nothing in her now of the wild, hot-tempered girl-next-door who had nearly run him off the dirt road yesterday, or of the sensuous femme fatale of last night, either. In their place stood a woman who looked every inch the cool, aloof, sophisticated lady Morgan had initially, before meeting her, supposed Cat to be. From her hair done up in a French twist to the stylish Bruno Magli pumps on her feet, this woman personified everything he had ever thought of as a "stuck-up Eastern broad." It struck him in that moment that Cat was, in fact, a carbon copy of Veronica Havers, the one woman he had ever been serious about, who had ditched him in the end for a suave financial investor.

The clever, flirtatious greeting that had sprung to Morgan's lips died unuttered.

"Good morning, Ms. Devlin," he said smoothly, coolly, instead. "If you're ready, you can get your father's Jeep and follow me to the dealership so we can get that damage to the front end squared away."

Cat was frankly puzzled—and not a little piqued and hurt—by his tone and by the fact that he had addressed her as "Ms. Devlin." After all, she had, finally, been "Cat" to him last night, had she not? Was this the same man who had called her only an hour ago and spoken to her so provocatively, tantalizing her? It did not appear so. Yet she could have sworn he had been glad to see her at first. What had happened to change that?

"Just let me get my handbag and lock up the house."

"Fine," Morgan replied tersely. "I'll wait for you outside."

He strode off without another word, leaving Cat staring after him, confused and now a little angry, too, before she closed the front door and made her way to the garage. From there, she backed the Jeep out into the driveway and then onto the street. As she did so, she happened to notice a battered old pickup truck parked alongside the curb a few doors down. Briefly, she frowned at the sight. From what she had seen so far of Vickridge, she knew instinctively the pickup did not belong in the neighborhood. But then she thought that perhaps the truck might be owned by one of the local yard services. She remembered seeing a couple of those around yesterday, their employees mowing lawns and weeding flower beds. She had made a mental note to herself at the time that she herself would need to engage such a service to maintain her father's own grounds if she planned on remaining in his house for any length of time. Otherwise, the grass would soon be waist high and the flower beds full of weeds. Something else to worry about. She supposed she would need a pool service, too. She sighed. There was certainly a lot more to taking care of a house than she had ever before realized—and something to be said for living in an apartment or a town house.

After glancing in his rearview mirror to make certain she was behind him, Morgan drove off in his Bronco. His earlier good mood was now so bad that he burned rubber as he sped away recklessly. Cat could think of nothing she had done to put him in such a foul temper, but whatever the cause, he had no right to take it out on her! she decided, incensed, as she raced after him. From firsthand experience yesterday, he knew she could not drive all that well, so just how did he expect her to keep up with him? Fortunately, this must have occurred to Morgan also, because shortly afterward, he slowed his speed. They turned south onto Rock Road, Cat just managing to get across the two lanes of oncoming traffic, which was at least a little lighter this morning than it had been yesterday afternoon. She glanced at her wristwatch. It was just after nine o'clock. Rush hour here in Wichita must be over, she mused gratefully, having dreaded the idea of trying to make her way through a horde of vehicles. Taxis, buses and subways she knew and could handle. Cars and trucks were another story.

At the busy intersection of Rock Road and what the bright green street sign announced was Kellogg, Morgan stopped at the red light, and as Cat eased the Jeep to a halt behind him, she observed that he was, by means of his rearview mirror, actually *glaring* at her! It was just too much! Her own temper rose accordingly, and for a crazy instant she was strongly tempted to bash his Bronco in the rear end. After all, the Jeep's front end was already damaged. But then common sense prevailed, and abruptly seized by another wild impulse, one that harkened back to childhood, she instead made a horrible face and stuck out her tongue at him. She saw his eyes widen in sheer surprise, and then, to her satisfaction, he laughed.

"Gotcha!" Cat mouthed to him, grinning.

Morgan had no time to mouth back any equally impudent reply, because just then the light changed from red to green. But as he turned west onto Kellogg, he discovered that his ill mood had vanished as suddenly as it had come upon him. He had been both amazed and amused by Cat's action—not in the least what he would have expected from a woman of her ilk. Not even in fun had Veronica Havers ever resorted to such childish behavior. He found it hard to believe Cat had. It was, however, a stunt Frank might have pulled; and in that moment Morgan realized that while his friend and business partner might be dead and gone, something of him remained behind in his daughter. It was somehow a comforting notion.

Cheered, Morgan pulled the Bronco into the Jeep dealership and parked. Then he walked back toward Cat as she drove in behind him.

"I owe you an apology," he said right off as she rolled down the window. "When I saw you this morning, I was . . . reminded of someone I'd prefer to forget, and I'm afraid I took it out on you. I was rude and wrong, and I'm sorry. What do you say we try this one last time—and get it right this time?" He held out his hand to her. "Ms. Devlin, I'm Morgan McCain, your father's friend and business partner, and I'm glad to meet you. Frank told me an awful lot about you over the years. He was mighty proud of you."

His explanation of his bad mood both enlightened and intrigued Cat. She had not given any thought to the notion that Morgan might already have a woman in his life. She was strangely glad to learn he did not, even as she thought ruefully that perhaps he was on the rebound, too. Still, he was man enough to admit a mistake and apologize for it, which spoke well of him. And his words about her father touched her deeply. It filled her with happiness to know her father had spoken of her, that he had been proud of her. Tears stung her eyes, although a smile, however tremulous, curved her lips as after a moment she slowly shook Morgan's outstretched hand.

"The pleasure's mine, Mr. McCain. Please...call me Cat."

"Only if you'll call me Morgan."

"That's a deal."

"No, that's a wrap! Cut. Print. There, you see? It might have required a few takes, but I knew we could get it right if only we tried. Pull the Jeep into that garage there—" he pointed toward the body shop "—and I'll meet you inside."

Once they had made the necessary arrangements for the repairs to the vehicle, Morgan escorted Cat to the Bronco. After opening the passenger door for her, he saw that she was comfortably settled inside before going around to slide into the driver's seat beside her.

"I noticed a flower shop—Tillie's, it was called—on the way here," Cat told him as he started up the vehicle. "Would you mind very much if we stopped there first? I'd—I'd like to take some flowers to—to Dad's grave."

"Of course...no problem," Morgan said kindly, silently cursing himself for having been such a cad earlier, for something that had not been Cat's fault and on the morning when she was to visit her father's grave for the first time besides. Morgan thought that if she now believed him to be an insensitive clod, he would have no one but himself to blame for it. Damn! Why was it that in the space of just two short days, the woman sitting beside him appeared to have effortlessly tangled him up in knots, so he now felt as though he did not know whether he was coming or going? Redheads. What was it about redheads?

At the flower shop Cat bought a simple but beautiful sheaf of gladiolus, which she loved but which she had also all her life associated with death and funerals. The scent of the bouquet filled the Bronco as Morgan drove her out east of town, to the cemetery where her father was buried. On the radio, adult-contemporary music played softly... four songs in a row before the deejay spoke and ran the commercials. She recognized the station as B98-FM, because that was its much-touted format.

"Somehow I rather expected you to be a fan of country-and-western music." Cat motioned toward the radio.

"Oh, I am," Morgan confirmed, glancing at her mockingly, as though he suspected she had thought him too much a cowboy to listen to anything else *but* country. "But that's good-time music—for wild days and even rowdier Saturday nights."

"In Margaritaville. Yes, I remember." Cat thought of his words to the two policemen last night. She shook her head disapprovingly, fighting to repress the smile that tugged at the corners of her lips at the memory. "Look, I don't mean to pry or anything... but are you—are you often hauled away to jail? I mean...Dad mentioned he'd bailed you out a couple of times in the past...."

"Yeah, once in a blue moon it's been known to happen, when I've got 'likkered up,' as they say, and got into a brawl at one of the local clubs." Morgan grinned at her sheepishly, a bad-boy grin that made Cat think that in his heart he was truly an outlaw. Then he confessed, "But that was mostly back in my *really* wild days! Now that I'm older and wiser, I'm not nearly as dangerous as I used to be. Too many young guns out there...just looking for an excuse to flatten an old man like me!"

"Uh-huh," Cat drawled sardonically, vividly conscious of the fact that he was not old at all, but a man plainly in his prime. "Wonder why it is, then, that I get the impres-

sion you could hold your own against just about anybody?''

''Probably because I can.'' Morgan flashed her another
grin—a smug one this time.

''Well, now we know modesty, at least, is not one of your
strong suits!''

''No, ma'am! I make no bones about it—I'm a straight
shooter. Right from the hip, too—and so I call 'em as I see
'em. Always have and always will.''

''You never learned then that honesty has to be mea-
sured out in small doses—and then only to those who can
take it?'' Cat inquired, arching one brow teasingly.

''Nope. If that's the medicine that'll cure you, I'll
cheerfully hog-tie you and spoon it forcibly down your
throat whether you want it or not.''

''Good heavens! I don't know whether I'm safe alone
with you or not!''

''You are . . . for the moment, at least. And should there
ever come a time when you're not, I'll let you know.'' From
beneath lazily hooded eyes, Morgan glanced at her in a way
that made Cat's heart pound suddenly hard and fast with
excitement.

''Will you?'' she asked, softly and a trifle breathlessly,
aware there was now a sensual note underlying their ban-
ter.

''Yes—and that's a promise.''

There was no time to pursue this particular conversation
further; they had reached the cemetery where her father was
buried. Briefly, Cat again felt a flash of guilt that she had
managed, even for a short while, to put her father's death
from her mind, to engage in a lighthearted flirtation while
she held in her lap the flowers for his grave. But in her heart
she knew her father would not have wanted her to feel sorrow for him. He had loved life, and he had lived it to its
fullest. He had wanted her to do the same, more than once
insisting—and rightly so, she realized now—that she had

buried herself in New York and in her work and in a round of social and charitable events.

"When was the last time you took a day off and just walked in the park, Cat?" he would ask her intently during his visits to New York. "New York's got beautiful parks...plenty of 'em. And what about that toy store...F.A.O. Schwarz? Why, if I lived here, I'd roam around in there once a month just to remind myself everybody ought to be a kid again now and then. You know, there *is* such a thing as being *too* adult, Cat. I'll bet that stuffed-shirt Spencer Kingsley doesn't even begin to know how to have fun...*real* fun, the kind that makes you laugh so hard that tears run down your cheeks. Bet he's never just plain silly."

No, Cat thought now as Morgan helped her down from the Bronco. Spence had never been just plain silly. She had never made a face and stuck her tongue out at him. Funny how she had not thought twice about doing that to Morgan McCain.

The cemetery, although lovely, was not what she had expected. It had no headstones in the traditional sense, only flat grave markers, so if Morgan had not accompanied her, she would have wandered around for a long while, searching for her father's grave. As it was, Morgan led her right to it. Despite the tears that filled her eyes at the sight, Cat could not help but smile as she gazed down at the gray, granite marker pressed into the rich, newly turned earth. In the center was engraved an oil derrick, framed by the words *Frank Devlin* and *The Best of the Wildcatters*, with the dates of his birth and death below. Shaking her head ruefully, Cat laughed softly.

"Oh, it's perfect. Dad would have loved it," she observed to Morgan, who stood at her side silently and a little defiantly, as though he had expected her to disapprove of the epitaph. She knelt to lay the sheaf of gladiolus tenderly upon her father's grave. Her fingers traced the words written in the granite. "Will you tell me about the service?" she asked. She had taken off the huge, tortoiseshell sunglasses she had donned earlier, and now her eyes squinted a little against the glare of the sunlight as she glanced up at Morgan earnestly.

To his surprise, he realized suddenly that he did not think he had ever seen a woman as beautiful as Cat appeared to him in that moment, kneeling there, her eyes slightly narrowed, glistening with tears, and as green and brilliant as emeralds. The sunlight danced upon her dark red hair, turning it to shimmering waves of upswept flame, and played across her porcelain skin, as lustrous as a pearl. Her moist, wine red mouth was parted in a tremulous smile that spoke of both grief at the loss of her father and gratitude that Morgan had known Frank so well, had, after all, done the right thing.

"Well, as you know," Morgan began quietly, "Frank wasn't much of a churchgoer, so we held the ceremony right here, at the grave side. It was a simple event, with a dignity all its own, although I suppose there are those who might have considered the eulogy I gave more fitting as an opening of 'The Tonight Show.' It *was* rather in the nature of something that might have been given at an Irish wake, actually. I spoke about Frank, about his life, about how he and I got started together in the oil-and-gas business, and I told about some of his wilder exploits. At any rate, it made people laugh, despite their tears, which I think would have pleased Frank, because he always said he didn't want anybody crying over him when he was dead and gone. Afterward the preacher spoke a few words... and quoted that 'dust to dust, ashes to ashes' passage from the Bible. Then, because Frank belonged to the Midian Shrine Temple, I had their bagpipers here to play 'Amazing Grace.' That was pretty much it."

"Thank you," Cat uttered simply. "I know Dad would have approved, because it sounds exactly like what he always insisted he wanted—'nothing fancy for a plain, good ole boy like me,' he used to say. I'm so sorry I couldn't get here in time, that I missed it. But I do have something of my own to add, if you don't mind." Slowly, she stood, opened her handbag and withdrew a folded sheet of paper. "It's an anonymous poem Dad and I both always liked. He used to say it summed up his entire philosophy about death and what happens to you afterward, where you go. I want to read it aloud, if I may."

"Please do," Morgan urged gently.

Cat cleared her throat. Then, after unfolding the paper, she began to read, her voice faltering a little over the simple but beautiful, uplifting words:

"Do not stand at my grave and weep....
I am not there. I do not sleep.

I am a thousand winds that blow.
I am the diamond glints on snow.
I am the sunlight on ripened grain.
I am the gentle autumn rain.
When you awake in the morning hush,
I am the swift, up-flinging rush
Of quiet birds in circling flight.
I am the soft star-shine at night.

Do not stand at my grave and cry....
I am not there. I did not die."

Having ended the poem, she fell silent, lost in her memories of her father. Then, after a long moment, she slowly folded the paper and returned it to her purse.

"'I am the sunlight on ripened grain,'" Morgan quoted softly, suddenly stricken. "That's what you were doing in the wheat field yesterday, isn't it? Searching for your father, for his essence, for whatever it was he meant to you. No wonder my shouting and honking made you so damned

mad. You must have thought I was the world's biggest
jerk—and now I feel like it, too! Worse, I feel like a real
heel! I am so sorry, Cat. I didn't know...I didn't realize...."

"I know you didn't, Morgan. And I'm not angry anymore. I feel pretty awful, too, actually, if you want to know
the truth. Mistaking you for a pervert, a stalker, and giving you that crack on the head last night. Why, I'd be willing to bet that wherever he is, Dad's having a great big
laugh at our expense right now!"

"Yeah, I can almost hear him! Frank was one of those
people who could always find the humor in any situation,
and who laughed, really *laughed*, you know, from the
belly."

And then somehow at that memory, Cat and Morgan
were both laughing, too. As she spied one of the cemetery's grounds keepers in the distance, she thought the man
must think they were crazy, standing there laughing in a
graveyard. Or perhaps he was old enough and sensitive
enough to understand that some things were just so painful that if you did not laugh, you would start crying and
never stop.

But after a while their laughter died away. Still, a trace of
companionship and joy remained, and Morgan's voice,
when he spoke, was now matter-of-fact.

"Do you like Mexican? Food, I mean. It's getting on toward lunchtime. I don't know about you, but I didn't have
any breakfast, and I'm hungry!"

"I adore Mexican," Cat answered, thinking that of all
the men in the world, it should have been Morgan who had
passed by her while she had stood in the wheat field, Morgan who had, during her reading of the poem just moments past, so quickly grasped what she had been doing
there yesterday, amid the acres of golden grain. Spence
would never have understood, she thought. He had com-

prehended things like profit-and-loss statements, not people's feelings.

She glanced down at her father's grave.

I love you, and I'll miss you, Dad, she told him silently. *But I hate goodbyes, and I've never believed death was the end, anyway, so I'll just say. . . until I see you again.*

Seven

Good Ole Boys

The restaurant was called Willie C's Café and Bar, and Cat knew, even before they went inside, that she was going to enjoy it. Its exterior sign was set into a grassy berm at the corner of the parking lot, and behind the sign itself lurked a cutout of a policeman on a motorcycle, hunched over the handlebars, poised to catch imaginary speeders. Sometimes the signboard cop was there and sometimes, he was not, Morgan explained, depending on whether he had been removed for repairs due to wear and tear.

The restaurant itself was one of those fun, trendy places with exposed pipes in the ceiling and old metal signs on the walls. Its claim to fame was its seemingly endless variety of beers from around the world. When the waitress came to their table, Cat and Morgan each, after glancing at the menu, ordered a bottle of dark beer and steak *fajitas*. The beers, when they arrived, were deliciously cold, the bottles dripping ice. While Cat and Morgan waited for their food, they sipped and talked.

"So...did you and Dad *really* name your corporation the One-Eyed Jacks Oil and Gas Company because you started it from your winnings one night at poker?" Cat asked, curious, never having quite believed this wild tale her father had told her.

"Yeah, believe it or not, we did." Morgan grinned at the memory. "It was one of those all-night, back-room games, because gambling, except for a couple of things like the lottery and betting on horse and dog races, is illegal in Kansas. Dawn was just breaking on the horizon, so we were down to the last hand, and since everybody there had been drinking all night long, the betting had got pretty crazy. There was a huge pot at stake. The game that round was five-card draw, and just to make it interesting, the dealer had announced that whoever held the jack with the ax was going to take half the pot, regardless. So even if you didn't win, you still had a chance at drawing the axman." He took a long swallow of beer, then went on.

"It was jacks or better to open—and that was all Frank had. Me...I was bust, didn't have anything worth looking at. Frank drew three cards and got nothing. I drew four and still didn't have anything—except for the last card I'd drawn, which just so happened to be the axman. So I'm running the pot up like crazy, and Frank's running it up, too, because he's putting on a big bluff, hoping to make the others think he's got an unbeatable hand. The next thing we knew, everybody else had dropped out, and it was just Frank and me. He had that pair of jacks—one of which was one-eyed—and I had the one-eyed axman. We split the pot, then pooled our winnings and started the company. Of course, it wasn't really all *that* simple, but we were on our way, at least."

"And now?"

"And now..." Morgan sighed heavily. "Now everything's up in the air until I find out how Frank's left his shares in the corporation. I'm sure he's willed them to you, Cat. We'll find out for certain this afternoon at Richard Hollis's office. But if he has, then the future of the One-Eyed Jacks Oil and Gas Company is going to be pretty much up to you."

"What do you mean? In what way?" Cat was puzzled, because she had thought that when her father and Morgan founded the corporation, they had doubtless made arrangements for the disposition of stock following the death of one partner. Now, however, it seemed from Morgan's words that perhaps they had not.

"Well, since you don't know anything about running an oil-and-gas company, and since you have a life in New York besides, you'll surely want to sell your shares, won't you, Cat?" Morgan prodded, on his tanned visage the expression he wore when playing poker, which was no expression at all and so revealed nothing of his own thoughts and emotions.

"Actually, to tell you the truth, I—I really haven't given Dad's will much thought," Cat confessed after a moment. "I mean...I'm not hard up for money or anything. My grandfather Talbot established a trust fund for me at my birth, and it's grown considerably through the years from a number of investments—besides which, I've never had any reason to touch the principal. So I've been very fortunate in that I've never had to struggle to earn a living. I've never been...you know...existing on my expectations from Dad's estate or anything. Didn't you and Dad have some sort of a buy-out agreement in place in the event of one partner's death?"

"Yes, of course." Morgan nodded. "But it's a first-option clause against the heir's—or heirs', if there are more than one—right to sell, and inheritance of the stock is subject to that condition. So...if Frank *did* will you his shares,

I'd have the first option to buy them if you chose to sell them. However, in the event that we couldn't come to terms, you'd be free to sell them elsewhere, or we could opt to dissolve the corporation and liquidate its assets."

"But—but that would mean the end of the One-Eyed Jacks Oil and Gas Company," Cat observed. "Of everything you and Dad worked so hard to build over the years. You surely wouldn't want that, Morgan, would you?"

"No, I wouldn't. Still, even that would be preferable to being compelled to deal fifty-fifty with someone who doesn't know beans about the oil-and-gas business."

By now their *fajitas* had arrived on steaming-hot, traditional cast-iron platters. Cat began studiously to spread sour cream on her tortilla, then to fill the tortilla itself with meat, onions, peppers, cheese, lettuce and tomatoes, ignoring only the guacamole, which she did not care for, having never acquired a taste for avocados.

"You don't like guacamole?" Morgan inquired as he watched her.

"No, not especially."

"Me, neither. There. I knew we were bound to have *something* in common."

"But not One-Eyed Jacks? Is that what you're saying?" She determinedly steered the conversation back to their previous topic, not knowing why it had suddenly become of such importance to her. Morgan was right: she had a life in New York and she knew nothing about the oil-and-gas business. Even so, she found herself protesting, "But I know about buying and selling, about importing and exporting."

"Furniture, antiques, paintings, objets d'art and other such stuff, yes. But not oil and gas," Morgan stated logically as he prepared his own *fajita,* also foregoing the guacamole on the side plate.

Cat shrugged, and her voice, when she replied, was confident, a shade defiant and accompanied by a stubborn, resolute lift of her chin.

"I could learn."

Morgan was silent for a moment, as though he were not quite sure what he was hearing. Then he spoke.

"What about your job in New York, Cat? And Frank had mentioned a boyfriend...a fiancé, now that I think about it." Morgan was abruptly stricken at the memory. He glanced down at her left hand. It was bare of jewelry. "But you're not wearing an engagement ring...?"

"No, I...broke off my engagement to Spence...Spencer Kingsley, my fiancé."

"Wasn't he also your boss or something? Didn't he own the firm where you worked?"

"Yes."

"Well, that must make your job pretty uncomfortable now, I would imagine," Morgan commented dryly, beginning to wonder where all this was leading.

"Actually, I—I...don't have a job anymore. Spence fired me."

"I see."

But the truth was Morgan did not see. He was, in fact, damned if he could figure out her agenda. Was Cat hinting that if Frank had indeed willed her his shares in the One-Eyed Jacks Oil & Gas Company, she intended to remain in Wichita, to step into his shoes at the corporation? Was she pumping him, Morgan, for information about the company so she could somehow attempt to wrest control of it from him, or was she merely interested in discovering what her shares were worth so she could sell them to him or to another investor? He did not know.

He thought suddenly of her background, of her education, of her professional experience, of the fact that she was accustomed to doing business in a city known for its ruthless corporate world, a city that was home to, among other things, Wall Street and Madison Avenue. Other than that, what did he *really* know about her? Upon learning her identity, he had thought she was nothing at all like what he had originally imagined. But what if he had not been so far off the mark after all? Morgan asked himself now, considering all the possible ramifications of having Cat herself as a fifty-fifty partner in the One-Eyed Jacks Oil & Gas Company.

Inwardly, he groaned at the idea. Not only would she prove a monumental distraction to him physically, but also, depending on her aims, either a flat-out nuisance or perhaps one of the cleverest and most dangerous opponents he had ever come up against. After all, she had had the wits, daring and composure to lie in wait for him in the dining room last night and, with that heavy vase, to coldcock him mercilessly, had she not? Perhaps she was actually as beautiful as belladonna. Veronica had been like that. Despite his attraction to Cat, he would have to be on his guard against her, Morgan decided now. To remember that even if she were Frank Devlin's daughter, she was also Julia Talbot's. Julia, who had kept from Frank his only child— and who had done her level best to poison Cat's mind against him.

"Look, I'm real sorry about your breakup and about your losing your job, Cat. But I'm sure that with your abilities, you won't have any trouble finding another position," Morgan asserted, because he would be damned if he'd tell her anything else about the One-Eyed Jacks Oil & Gas Company now, reveal anything that might help her with whatever plans she had in mind—at least not until he discovered whether he must really consider her a threat. He would not be made a fool of again, as Veronica had made a fool of him. It might be that Cat's broken engagement and her firing were somehow related. Perhaps she had attempted to boss Spencer Kingsley around, to grab control of *his* company—and that was what had led to the breakup of her engagement and her subsequent firing, because what man worth his salt would tolerate being dictated to by a woman?

"Oh, I can always find another job," Cat agreed easily, oblivious of Morgan's current thoughts. "It's establishing a *career* that's the hard part. There really is a glass ceiling women come up against in business, you know, a prejudice against our climbing any higher than a few token upper-management positions in the corporate world. We still earn only approximately seventy cents for a man's every dollar—and I think that far too often, we have to work twice as hard as a man to get it, too!"

"That's what you think, is it?" Morgan eyed her skeptically. Damn! A feminist, to boot—and just when, half ashamed of and disgusted by his suspicions, he had almost convinced himself they were unwarranted, that because of his bad experience with Veronica, he was once more and without any good reason leaping to conclusions about Cat.

"Well, it's true, isn't it?" Cat probed, only half teasingly.

Reluctantly, Morgan was compelled to admit it was. After that, however, although she made more than one attempt to continue their conversation, he was strangely taciturn. She did not know what had prompted this new change in his obviously mercurial moods, but she could not help but remember what he had told her earlier—that she reminded him of someone he would prefer to forget.

At that thought, some of Cat's pleasure in their lunch went out of her day, and she was quiet and reflective while Morgan paid their bill, then led her outside to the Bronco. After she was comfortably settled inside, he drove downtown, and she got her first glimpse of the heart of city, which, upon her arrival in Wichita, the taxi driver had avoided by taking her along the meandering Big and Little Arkansas rivers and through various park areas.

The city was small and simple but beautiful, many of its main intersections paved with old-fashioned brick, the sidewalks lined with trees. No building was taller than twenty-six stories, so the skyline was much lower than that of New York, and sunlight slanted down brightly.

Along the way, Morgan pointed out a number of sites to her, among them Naftzger Park and, across the street from that, a pseudohistorical district he said was called Old Town. It reminded her a little, somehow, of the South Street Seaport in New York, with all its shops and restaurants and its turn-of-the-century Victorian air. Here again old-fashioned bricks paved the streets, which were studded with reproduction lampposts and park benches, and there were large, pleasant parking lots to accommodate all the cars.

"I'll bring you down here one evening if you like," Morgan offered as he pulled into one of the Old Town parking lots, "show you some of the city's nightlife." He deftly maneuvered the Bronco into an empty space, then shut off the motor. "Richard Hollis's office is a few blocks from here, but with your being from New York, I didn't think you'd mind if we walked. It's a nice day, and I know ten blocks or more is nothing to a New Yorker."

Cat was glad to see that the mischievous twinkle had returned to his eyes and that his increasingly familiar, crooked grin curved his mouth when he looked over at her.

"That's right," she replied, smiling. "How do you think I stay in such great shape?" She had intended the remark only to be flippant, but as his suddenly heated eyes roamed over her lingeringly, she could not prevent the blush that rose to her cheeks.

"You are definitely that," he agreed appreciatively, wondering what she would think if he told her that in her peach-colored linen suit, she somehow reminded him of a crystal glass of sorbet, that he could almost taste her melting on his tongue. Instead, he forced himself to glance away, pretending to check his wristwatch. "Well, we've got just about fifteen minutes before our appointment with Richard Hollis. So we'd better get a move on."

Once they reached the sidewalk, Cat noticed that Morgan moved around her instinctively so he was curbside—a holdover from previous centuries, when a gentleman always walked on the outside so a lady would not be drenched by the contents of slop jars emptied from upper-story windows. The courtesy seemed somehow quaint in this day and age. Yet it was still the mark of a man with manners, and Cat appreciated the gesture. Even if he *were* a rough-diamond cowboy, Morgan did, after all, have a few smooth edges, it seemed.

"Oh, look! A trolley!" she exclaimed suddenly, laughing aloud with a child's delight as the vehicle trundled past them.

"It's a bus, actually," Morgan corrected, "although it does resemble the old trolleys that did, in fact, used to run here. You can still see the tracks in places. But these days we get the same picturesque effect without all the hassle."

"Well, I still think it's charming and romantic," she insisted.

"Then we'll have to take a ride on one sometime."

"That sounds nice—but, well . . . look, Morgan, I don't want you to feel obligated to show me the city sights or otherwise entertain me while I'm here in Wichita. I assure you I'm a big girl now, and I've been used to taking care of myself for a long, long time, besides."

Although Cat had striven for a lighthearted tone, Morgan believed he detected a tiny note of bitterness in her last words, nevertheless. For the first time, he wondered what her life, her childhood, must have been like, growing up in the Talbot family mansion and without her father. Instinctively, Morgan sensed that Julia Talbot had not been the closest and most loving and nurturing of mothers. It further occurred to him how often a crowded city like New

York could, perversely, emphasize one's own loneliness and isolation. Although Cat had had her family, her fiancé and her work to occupy her, she might in reality have been close to no one. Perhaps even her friends had been more in the nature of business and social acquaintances, as was so frequently the case in the corporate world, rather than true, cross-your-heart-and-hope-to-die friends. There was, he had come gradually to realize, a strange, appealing vulnerability in her that he would not usually have associated with a woman of her ilk.

Morgan's own family had loved him, and Frank had treated him like a son. But now he recognized that perhaps Cat had been alone, even unloved, until adulthood, when Frank and she had set about establishing the relationship they ought to have shared all their lives. Was it any wonder then she had loved her father so deeply?

"I don't feel any obligation toward you whatsoever, Cat," Morgan declared in response to her earlier remarks. "So if I take you anywhere or do anything for you, you can rest assured it's because I want to and not because I feel as though I have to. I just thought that since you made the trip here to Wichita, especially when you didn't have to, you'd like to see some of the things I know Frank was planning to show you this summer." Morgan paused for moment, gathering his thoughts. Then he continued.

"Look, Cat, I know that, culturally, Wichita can't begin to compete with New York. But we're not totally backwoods here, either. You see that big round building over there?" He pointed to a huge, sand-colored, circular edifice in the distance, rising from the beautifully landscaped edge of the riverbank, and Cat nodded. "That's Century Two, which contains our convention and exhibition halls, as well as one of our live theaters, where you can see productions to rival anything off or *on* Broadway. Musicals are perennially popular here. Robert Goulet performed in *Camelot* at Century Two not too long ago—although I *did* wonder how he felt about playing King Arthur now, when he'd originated the role of Lancelot! As for ballet, well, Gelsey Kirkland has danced *The Nutcracker* there. We've got some awfully fine art in Wichita, too. Just look around you—'' his hand swept out, indicating various sculptures on the streets ''—and what you see here is equaled or surpassed by what's out at Wichita State University, where the art building alone has a rare mural by Miró on its front. Nor will you see any better Native American art anywhere. Blackbear Bosin's statue *The Keeper of the Plains,* at the confluence of the Big and Little Arkansas rivers, is magnificent.''

''Morgan McCain! Are you trying to tell me I'm a snob—or provincial?'' Cat inquired tartly.

''No, neither. I'm just saying Frank wanted you to realize Manhattan Island is not the beginning and end of the world.''

''I know that. But it sure is exciting . . . much more fast paced than downtown Wichita, for example,'' she retorted, pride demanding she defend her hometown.

''Yes, it is that, I agree. But there's something to be said for life in the slow lane, too. Frank just wanted you to know that.'' By now they had reached an office building, and Morgan opened one of the heavy glass front doors, ushering Cat into the marble-floored lobby and then toward the bank of elevators in the hallway beyond.

''Don't we have to . . . you know . . . sign in or anything?'' she asked, glancing around at her surroundings as she and Morgan waited for one of the elevators' doors to open.

He grinned at her. ''Like I said, this isn't New York, Cat—although, even here, most of these buildings *do* keep their rest rooms locked!''

She frowned at him with mock reproval. ''Aha! So Wichita isn't quite a paradise after all. Is that what you're telling me?''

"Pretty proud of yourself for figuring that out so quick, despite all my efforts to convince you otherwise, aren't you? Yes, it's true—but then, you aren't likely to be mugged on the streets here, either! Now get in the elevator, woman. If the truth were known, you're probably a worse menace to Wichita society than one of the local winos or panhandlers!"

Taking her elbow before she could retort, Morgan steered her past the brass-plated doors that had just glided open. Inside, he pressed the button for the fourth floor, and they rode up in silence, Cat pretending studiously, after his last remark, to ignore him. Whistling under his breath, Morgan watched her openly, not troubling to repress the smile that tugged at his lips or the admiration in his eyes as they traveled over her.

"You look like a peach in that outfit," he commented at last, with feigned nonchalance, "and I'll just bet you're as tasty as one, too. You'd better not sit too close to Hollis in his office . . . he's the kind liable to take a bite out of you."

Cat was not normally at a loss for words. But before she could think of a suitable rejoinder, Morgan had escorted her into the legal firm and was announcing their names to the receptionist just inside. After speaking into her telephone for a moment, the woman announced that Mr. Hollis would be with them shortly and suggested they have a seat in the meanwhile. Cat settled herself on the reception room's comfortable, overstuffed love seat, somehow agitated when, instead of taking a chair, Morgan sat beside her, his thigh pressing hers almost intimately—and, she half suspected, deliberately, although it was hard to be sure. The love seat was not very wide, and its cushions were so soft and plump that Cat and Morgan both sank into them. He draped his arm over the back of the love seat, too, just brushing her shoulders. For an instant she had a sudden, wild urge to lay her head back, to move into the curve of his

body, to feel his arms wrapped around her, holding her safe
and secure.

But of course, she did no such thing—especially when
she spied the receptionist eyeing her and Morgan surreptitiously, clearly speculating on what, if anything, might be
between them. Still, Cat could not suppress the unexpected flash of pride and satisfaction, the inexplicable
twinge of jealousy and possessiveness that shot through her
at the idea that the receptionist found Morgan attractive—
and that she, Cat, should, however mistakenly, be perceived as his woman. Despite herself, she had to admit it
was a boost to her ego, particularly after her falling-out
with Spence. He had been considered quite a catch by their
circle of friends and acquaintances, most of whom had
thought Cat was a fool for breaking off her engagement to
him.

But however flattering and gratifying the momentary il-
lusion of a relationship between her and Morgan, Cat was
nevertheless relieved when her father's attorney made his
appearance. Sitting so close to Morgan, she had been vividly aware of his masculinity, of his strength, of the subtle
scents of soap and cologne and sweat that emanated from
his tanned flesh, involuntarily making her remember the
sound of his voice on the telephone earlier that morning,
and of how she had wondered afterward if he had been lying—naked—in bed when he had called her. So powerful,
in fact, was that image as it rose unbidden in her mind that
she was barely aware of Morgan introducing her to Richard Hollis. It was only at the lawyer's complimentary but
slyly suggestive remarks that she was jolted from her reverie into the realization that Morgan had perhaps been
right, that Mr. Hollis *was* indeed the kind of man who
could be expected, if not to take a bite out of her, at least
to pinch covertly a woman's derrière. Instinctively, she
edged a little closer to Morgan, only to find herself scowling at him and longing to slap the smug smirk off his face

when he mouthed, "I told you so," behind Mr. Hollis's back as the lawyer turned to lead them toward his office. She gave Morgan what she hoped was a quelling glare, but it had no visible effect upon him, except to cause him to grin even wider as they followed the congenially chatting attorney.

Still, to her relief, once seated in front of Mr. Hollis's desk, waiting silently but expectantly as he sorted through his papers to withdraw what Cat knew must be her father's last will and testament, Morgan became abruptly all-business. She sensed rather than observed the tension that coiled within him at that moment, so that despite his outwardly calm and relaxed demeanor, she somehow knew he was as alert and wary as a predator. It occurred to her then that he was really not so easygoing as he seemed, that he did have a black temper, that there was possibly a dangerous, maybe even deadly aspect to Morgan's character—and that if her father had willed her his shares in the One-Eyed Jacks Oil & Gas Company, she might be about to see that dark side.

Involuntarily, Cat shuddered at the thought. Her every business instinct warned her she did not want to tangle with Morgan McCain. That, just like her, he went for broke and played to win.

Mr. Hollis began to read her father's will aloud, stopping now and then to explain or elaborate upon a point as he turned the crisp white pages stapled into the traditional blue legal cover. Once he'd finished, Cat sat there for a moment in silence, stunned. Then, her temper rising as she grasped the import of her father's decision, but wanting to be entirely clear about it, she spoke.

"Mr. Hollis—"

"Rich...please, call me Rich, Ms. Devlin," the lawyer drawled.

"Very well...Rich, then. Are you telling me that although my father left me forty-eight percent of his shares in the One-Eyed Jacks Oil and Gas Company, the two percent that he willed to Morgan has given *him* controlling interest in the corporation?"

"Yes, yes, that's the upshot of it exactly, Ms. Devlin." The attorney nodded briskly. "You're an astute woman, I can tell. Still, let's face it—you don't know anything about running an oil-and-gas company, as I'm sure Frank was well aware. So, giving you the power to stalemate any decisions Morgan might want to make with regard to the corporation would hardly have been fair now, would it? After all, along with Frank, Morgan founded the One-Eyed Jacks Oil and Gas Company. He built it over the years into the successful entity it's become. This way it can continue along those lines, under Morgan's aegis, with you still benefiting from Frank's own investment in the company—and, I might add, Ms. Devlin, with your not being compelled to trouble your pretty head about business matters that surely wouldn't have been of any interest to you, in any event."

At that, it was all Cat could do to restrain herself from exploding, although, in fact, she did not know why she was so damned mad. She had not expected her father to leave her anything, much less the bulk of his estate, including the majority of his shares in the One-Eyed Jacks Oil & Gas Company. Indeed, that he had done so should have gladdened her heart, because it was surely proof of how much she had meant to him. And certainly, ensuring that Morgan, his friend and business partner, had gained controlling interest in the corporation was, as Mr. Hollis had already so logically pointed out, only fair. Still, Cat could not repress the irrational feelings of pique and hurt that rose within her at the thought that no matter how much her father had loved her, he plainly had not trusted her ability to follow in his footsteps at the One-Eyed Jack Oil & Gas Company, either.

Well, and why should he have? she tried to ask herself reasonably. Although she had often chatted with her father about his work, she had never expressed any serious interest in learning about it. She had never indicated she would be willing to give up her life and job in New York to move to Wichita, to take a position in his corporation, with the understanding that he would be training her to step into his shoes upon his retirement or at his death. As a result, she had no cause whatsoever to feel slighted. Yet the incontrovertible fact was she did. It was silly and childish, but there it was all the same—and the smile of satisfaction that now curved Morgan's mouth only made Cat's indignation worse. She knew he was inwardly ecstatic not to have been saddled with her as a fifty-fifty partner, ecstatic to have gained controlling interest in the corporation.

Damn it! She was an intelligent, competent, professional businesswoman, confident of her capability to make a success of most anything she chose to put her mind to. That her father and Mr. Hollis, and possibly Morgan, had conspired to rob her of that opportunity was galling and painful. They were men, and they had doubted her, probably—if Mr. Hollis's attitude were any indication—for no better reason than that she was a woman!

Cat believed that deep down inside, regardless of how outwardly liberal any of them might appear, all men harbored macho tendencies, secretly felt themselves to be superior to women. Spence surely had. It was his questioning of her opinion over a purchase for the import-export firm that had led to their terrible argument, which he had ended abruptly with the supercilious statement that he was a man and that, as such, he fully intended to wear the pants in their relationship, both professionally and personally. Incensed by his high-handed dismissal of her judgment, by his pigheaded refusal even to consider she might be right about the acquisition for the firm, Cat had, in the heat of the moment, broken off their engagement. Stung by her rejection, Spence had then coldly informed her she was permitting her personal feelings to interfere with her professional duties, that an invariably emotional response to business matters was why all females were unsuited for top-management positions. He had then suggested that, this being the case, perhaps Cat ought to search for a less-demanding job, one where her bouts of PMS would not prove so disruptive to the orderly, rational workings of the male corporate world.

That had been so low a blow that Cat had not trusted herself to speak further. Instead, with every ounce of will-power she possessed, she had forced herself to clamp her jaws shut and turn and walk away without another word. She had rarely ever suffered from premenstrual syndrome—and she had certainly never, for any cause, behaved irresponsibly on the job. She had hoped and counted on the fact that with their marriage she and Spence would become partners in the import-export firm. Instead, she had found her head slammed against the glass ceiling he himself had erected above her.

Now she felt herself striking another one in Mr. Hollis's office. That she knew nothing about the oil-and-gas industry was irrelevant. She was not stupid, and she ought at least to have been permitted the chance to learn, to prove herself before judgment had been passed upon her. That Mr. Hollis was leering at her from behind his desk only further outraged her. He was unquestionably a sharp lawyer, or her father would not have employed him. But his manner toward women left much to be desired. Cat had no doubt that if Morgan had not been present, Rich Hollis would by now be well on his way to chasing her around his office, wilily passing off his advances as comforting gestures of sympathy for her loss. That because she was a woman she should require the presence of another man to forestall such indignities was the acid icing on an already-bitter cake.

"Thank you for your clarification of that last point, Mr. Hollis," she said as coolly as she could manage, struggling to master her anger. "Now, if you'll just show me what, if any, documents need to be signed, I will be able to settle my father's estate and not be compelled to take up any more of your valuable time."

"I'm sure I don't need to remind you I'm being well paid for that time, Ms. Devlin . . . Cat." The smile the attorney gave her reminded her of the proverbial fox licking its chops. "However, I can understand your wanting to get matters wrapped up as soon as possible, since you do, after all, have a life in New York. I imagine Doo-dah—that's how we less-provincial locals refer to Wichita—must seem pretty tame and boring to a big-city gal like you. I know I always have to set my watch back at least a decade when I return home from a trip out of town," he declared, only half-jokingly. "So why don't I have my secretary draw up the necessary paperwork by tomorrow morning, and you can either stop by my office to sign on all the dotted lines, or I can have it mailed to you, whichever you prefer." The expression on Mr. Hollis's face left her no doubt as to his own preference.

"Please send it to my father's home address." Cat smiled, falsely sweet, as she rose to her feet, suppressing the urge to snatch away her hand rudely as the lawyer reached out to shake it.

As he ushered them to the door of his office, Mr. Hollis shook Morgan's hand, too, and jovially clapped him on the shoulder, congratulating him on his good fortune. Shortly afterward, Cat and Morgan stood in the hallway outside the legal firm, waiting for an elevator to take them back down to the lobby.

"I simply do *not* understand how my father could have employed such a man," Cat remarked in the silence, her brow knit with disapproval and annoyance.

"Who...Rich?" Morgan quirked one eyebrow upward, grinning at her scowl. "Well, I *did* warn you, didn't I? But don't let him fool you. He may act like he barely scraped through law school, but the truth is he's about as shrewd as attorneys come. It's not his fault he's also a good ole boy with a weakness for anything in skirts."

"Isn't it?" Cat retorted sourly.

"Why, no, darlin'," Morgan drawled, grinning even more hugely at her. "It's the nature of the beast. Some of us are just a little more subtle and a great deal more selective about it than others—although I admit that I would find it hard to fault Rich's eye this afternoon."

"You know, Morgan, you're real lucky there's a floor in there." Cat pointed to the elevator as it clanged to a stop before them and the brass-plated doors slid open. "Otherwise, the way I feel right now, I'd have been sorely tempted to shove you down the shaft!"

His laughter rang in her ears. Yet somehow, despite that, despite everything, she could not halt the sudden, hard thudding of her heart at the unmistakable desire in his glance and at the thought that he had called her "darlin'." Silently, Cat cursed herself for a fool, but it did not help. And all the way down to the lobby, she was discomfited by a wild, unbidden and inexplicable fantasy in which Morgan suddenly pressed her up against one wall of the elevator, pushed her linen skirt up around her thighs and took her urgently in a mutual burst of savage, uncontrollable passion before, outwardly calm and collected, they exited the car.

Eight

Chemistry . . . the Equalizer

The next few days Cat spent pacing the rooms of her father's house and thinking endlessly, feeling somehow as though she had reached a crossroads, a turning point in her life. For the first time she could remember since childhood, she found herself with time hanging heavily on her hands, with neither school nor a job nor social and charitable engagements to occupy her hours. She had no university classes, no business meetings and no functions of any sort to attend, no deadlines to meet, no appointments to keep, no one to see and no place to go.

For the space of a single day, it was heavenly.

Rather than rising early, she luxuriated in sleeping late. Instead of coffee and a bagel snatched on the run, she ate a leisurely breakfast, lingering over the stock-market section of the daily newspaper, the *Wichita Eagle*. She took a long shower and washed her hair, after which she gave her-

self a facial, a manicure and a pedicure. She swam in the
pool out back and caught up on some of her reading. She
watched television and, later that evening, continued the
task of sorting through her father's personal papers and
belongings, boxing everything up and labeling it neatly with
black, felt-tipped markers.

But by the following afternoon, accustomed to long,
hard hours of work, Cat was already bored out of her
mind, stir-crazy, practically climbing the walls of her father's house. She wondered how her mother had been sat-
isfied to spend her whole life as a social butterfly, attending
lunches and brunches, playing bridge, tennis and golf at the
local country club and patronizing this social or charitable
event or that. With time just to think, to dwell on, among
other things, her relationship with Spence, Cat now realized that far from envisioning her as a partner in the import-export firm, he had seen her, following their marriage,
as stepping into her mother's shoes instead. Too late Cat
recognized that he had said as much on more than one occasion. Wrapped up in her career and her own plans for
their future, she had simply chosen not to hear him, had
chosen to delude herself into believing he would come
around to her point of view once he understood how very
important it was to her.

She would *not*, however, she assured herself as she
walked back to her father's house from the mailbox at the
end of the driveway, make that same mistake with Morgan
McCain. Him she had heard loud and clear. He did not
want as his partner in the One-Eyed Jacks Oil & Gas Company someone who knew nothing about the oil-and-gas
business. Well, that was just fine and dandy with her, Cat
reflected crossly as she ripped open the big envelope from
Richard Hollis's office and thought again of her father's
will, of how he had disposed of his shares in the corporation. She would sell Morgan the forty-eight percent of her
father's stock she had inherited and be done with it! Then

she would kick Wichita's prairie dust off her heels and head back to the big city, to the real world of New York, where she belonged.

That she no longer had anything, truly, to return to there—no job, no fiancé, no real family and only a few friends—was immaterial. It was her home. That her father had always insisted home is wherever one's heart is, was a thought Cat determinedly shoved from her mind. Despite how much he had loved her, even *he* had not trusted her to follow in his footsteps at the One-Eyed Jacks Oil & Gas Company, had made it clear with the disposition of his shares that he had not expected her to do so.

Once inside the house, Cat made her way to her father's study, where she read and then signed all the documents Richard Hollis had enclosed in the envelope. Then she sat down at her father's laptop computer to compose a letter to Morgan, offering for sale her shares in the One-Eyed Jacks Oil & Gas Company, per the terms of the corporation's buy-out agreement. Then, before she could change her mind, she sealed the envelope, stamped it and drove to the nearest post-office drop box to mail it.

"Forgive me if I seem inordinately slow or confused this morning, but...what do you mean, you can't raise the capital to buy my stock?" Cat's brow was knit with puzzlement as she gazed at Morgan across her father's kitchen table. They had just come back from the Jeep dealership, to which Morgan had driven her earlier to pick up her vehicle, which was now repaired. Knowing from his telephone call of a few days ago that he had received her letter about her wanting to sell him her shares in the One-Eyed Jacks Oil & Gas Company, she had invited him back for coffee and to discuss her offer.

"Just that...just exactly what I said, Cat—there's no way at the moment I can put together the necessary financing to buy you out," Morgan reiterated, slightly defensive and embarrassed. After all his talk to her about not wanting her as a partner in the corporation, it was humiliating to be forced to admit he himself was not in a position to do anything about it, that he could not take her up on her offer, no matter how much he might wish to do so. Nor were matters helped by the fact that she was, this morning, dressed in a simple T-shirt and a pair of plain old jeans, reminding him of how she had looked at their first meeting, of how much he had wanted her in that instant. Inwardly, Morgan groaned. Whether he liked it or not, Cat continued to play havoc with his senses! Every time he glanced at her it was as though he could think of nothing but sleeping with her! It made him feel as though he had regressed to his days as a hormone-driven teenager, was not now a mature man who ought to have better control over himself and a good deal more common sense! "Look, Cat, you've got to understand that the oil-and-gas business is in kind of a bad way right now—"

"Why is that…when you showed profits just a few years back?" she interrupted, oblivious of his unbusinesslike thoughts, letting him know she had done her homework, that to prepare herself for this discussion, she had read, among other things, the corporation's most-recent annual reports.

"Yes, but that was during Desert Storm. As horrible and unconscionable as it might seem, Cat," Morgan explained dryly, "American oilmen, among others, benefited when Iraq swooped down to invade Kuwait and set the Kuwaiti oil fields on fire. With Kuwait burning, and various of the other OPEC nations tied up in the Gulf War besides, oil shipments from the Middle East were curtailed. And since the Arab nations are the world's primary suppliers of oil, that drove the price of oil up worldwide, which meant that North and South American oil companies, for example, made money. Once that situation had ended, things more or less returned to the way they've been for the last several years." He paused for a moment. Then he continued.

"You surely must have some idea of how, practically overnight it seemed, the bottom dropped out of the oil market some years back, Cat, and how cities like Houston and Tulsa, whose economies were fueled by that oil, were left up the financial creek until they could begin attracting and developing other industries. The *Exxon Valdez* incident off the coast of Alaska didn't help matters, either. It stirred up not only the environmentalists, but also the entire country—although not without just cause, mind you . . . so you needn't go getting up in arms about it yourself! And don't say you weren't, because I could practically see your hackles rising! Believe it or not, I share your concerns, so I'm certainly not about to sit here and defend oil companies that either deliberately or carelessly damage this planet. Still, the fact remains that the American oil business is no longer the booming industry it was in its heyday."

"I see." Cat chewed her lower lip thoughtfully, unaware of the effect this simple gesture produced upon Morgan, of how, as he watched her, he longed to nibble that sultry, sensuous lip himself, and so found that he could hardly concentrate on their conversation. "What you're saying is that, barring another crisis in the Middle East or some other turn of events, the oil industry is more or less bust at the moment, and as a result, you can't get your bank to extend you any credit."

"No, not precisely." Morgan shook his head, as though that action might clear his thoughts of their decidedly sexual drift. With difficulty he forced his mind back to the discussion at hand, knowing how important it was to the future of the One-Eyed Jacks Oil & Gas Company. "I'm saying that in order to do this deal, I'd either have to liquidate other assets I hold or else put them up as collateral against loans I'd rather not take out right now to begin with, because it just isn't smart ever to put all your eggs in one basket.''

''Then, under the circumstances, it's probably not too likely that any other investor will want to buy my shares in the corporation, either, is it?'' Cat queried, frowning as she mulled over the issue—slowly, unwittingly, running her forefinger back and forth across her lower lip as she contemplated her limited options.

''Frankly, no,'' Morgan answered tersely. ''In fact, if you want my advice, you'd be wise to hang on to your stock until the price of oil goes up again, at which time you might make a killing on the market.''

''And let you run the company in the meanwhile, however you see fit?''

''Well . . . yes, Cat. We've been over this before, and I thought we'd agreed that you sure as heck don't know anything about it.''

''If you remember correctly, I also said I could learn.'' Abruptly, Cat ceased the unconscious, erotic rubbing of her lower lip and sat up straighter in her chair, her chin lifting stubbornly, her eyes flashing with challenge and defiance, her decision made. ''And seeing as how it's just not in my nature to be either a hypocrite or a parasite, if I *am* going to be a partner—even a minority partner—in the One-Eyed Jacks Oil and Gas Company, then a partner I fully intend to be! What time did my father usually arrive at his office in the mornings?''

''Between seven and eight o'clock, but—''

''Then you may expect me there tomorrow morning at the same time.'' Her heart pounding at the darkening expression on Morgan's face, she stood, indicating the door. ''Thank you for taking me to retrieve the Jeep, Morgan. But now, if you don't mind, I've got a lot of work to do, and I'm sure you must be busy as well.''

''Cat . . .'' His voice was low, deceptively silky, but she was not fooled. She knew he was suddenly as angry as she had been some days ago in Richard Hollis's office. "What do you think you're doing, Cat? If you believe for one single minute that I'm going to let you just walk in and try to take over One-Eyed Jacks—"

"Who said anything about my taking it over? I merely intend to pull my weight, that's all. And you don't have any right to attempt to prevent me from doing that, Morgan— legal or otherwise. I don't believe in taking something for nothing. If I could have sold my shares in the corporation, it might have been different. But I'm accustomed to managing my own business affairs and investments, and whether you like it or not, as a forty-eight-percent stockholder in One-Eyed Jacks, I have obligations to the corporation that go beyond my just sitting around collecting a check I don't need and I didn't earn to begin with!"

"Even if I don't want you at the office?" Morgan prodded as he, too, rose to his feet, no longer looking in that instant like an easygoing cowboy, Cat thought nervously, but rather like some kind of dangerous predator uncoiling himself and preparing to pounce—on her! Involuntarily, she took a step back, her pulse leaping.

"You don't want me there because I'm a woman, damn it!" she protested, fighting to control the abrupt impulse she had to turn and run from the kitchen before whatever ominous, explosive thing she now belatedly sensed brewing between them erupted.

"Well, boy howdy, you got that right!" he retorted.

"So...you admit it! That *is* a surprise. But then I already knew it, so you couldn't have fooled me anyway, even if you'd tried! You think that just because I'm a woman, I can't do the job, and you don't even want to give me the chance to try! And that's so shortsighted and bullheaded and unfair of you! Oh, you're no better than Spence...just another macho man, a male chauvinist pig who thinks women ought to be kept barefoot and pregnant—"

"You'd be wise to hold off on your hotheaded insulting
of me until you get your facts straight, Cat." Morgan's
voice was quiet but lethal, and it sent a shiver of both apprehension and inexplicable anticipation coursing through
her as he moved toward her, slowly backing her up against
the kitchen counter and placing his hands on either side of
her so she could not escape. "I *do* question your ability to
do the job, but *that* has nothing to do with your being a
woman!"

"Then . . . I—I don't understand. What—what has my
gender got to with it at all then?"

"This."

Before Cat realized what he intended, Morgan caught
hold of her, his strong hands burrowing through her dark
red hair, deliberately compelling her face up to his. His
mouth came down on hers, speaking silently, urgently, of
his hunger for her. Taken by surprise, she acquiesced to his
kiss, feeling as though the earth had suddenly heaved, had
dropped without warning from beneath her feet as he
molded her to him. His hands tightened in her hair as he
slanted his lips over hers, his mustache tickling her, his
tongue tracing the outline of her mouth before parting it,
thrusting inside, deepening the kiss, exploring the warm,
dark cavern of her.

Deep down inside Cat, desire flickered, the spark flaring
quickly and uncontrollably into a flame that swept through
her like wildfire, consuming her, as she had somehow
sensed it would should Morgan ever touch her, kiss her,
make love to her. Of their own volition, her arms crept up
his muscular chest, fingers splayed and trembling with the
onslaught of passion before they clutched his broad shoulders, nails biting into his flesh, spurring him on as he took
her mouth again and again, hotly, eagerly demanding her
response.

She moaned low in her throat as his hands slid down her
back, provocatively kneading her spine before cupping her

buttocks, pressing her against him so she could feel the heat and strength of his arousal. Her knees went weak. She felt as though she were melting, trickling down into a pool of mindless sensation at his feet, and in some dark corner of her mind, she was startled to grasp dimly that she was still standing. She knew it was only because Morgan held her up as his lips burned from her mouth to the pulse fluttering crazily at the delicate hollow of her throat.

Then, at long last, with a low groan of reluctance, he drew away, his eyes like blue fire as he stared down at her, his glance taking in the tangle he had made of her hair; the quiver of her tremulous, parted lips, slightly bruised from his kisses; the rapid, shallow rise and fall of her breasts beneath the butter yellow T-shirt she wore; the sight of her pebbled nipples straining tautly against the thin cotton.

"I have been wanting to do that from the very first moment I saw you, Cat." Morgan's voice was husky with the desire that roiled within him. "And that's the real reason I don't want you at the office. I don't think I'll be able to think clearly with you there, and it's been my experience, besides, that mixing business with pleasure seldom works out. Most people just can't separate their personal feelings from their professional responsibilities."

If Cat had been dazed from his kisses, his words served like a bucket of cold water rudely thrown in her face, abruptly restoring her to her senses. For had not Spence said much the same thing to her during their argument, accused her of letting her emotions get in the way of her job—when in reality it had been *he* who could not keep his love and business lives apart?

"You needn't worry about that, Morgan," she insisted as coolly as she could manage, wishing her heart would stop thudding so fast in her breast, that her breathing would return to normal. "Because if you forget at the office, I'll be sure to remind you."

"Then you're really serious about coming to work at One-Eyed Jacks?"

"Yes ... yes, I am," she responded obstinately.

Morgan was silent for a long, tense moment, staring at her intently, his dark visage still, closed, unreadable, revealing nothing of his thoughts and emotions. Then, with a low growl of what might have been displeasure, despair, defiance or all three, he turned away, grabbing his Stetson from the table and clapping it roughly on his head.

"Have it your way then. But be warned, Cat." His eyes traveled over her blatantly, lingering on her lush mouth, her swollen breasts. "You are no longer safe alone with me!"

Then he strode from the kitchen, deliberately slamming the front door behind him.

After he had gone, Cat leaned against the kitchen counter weakly, still shaking from the aftermath of her emotions, the sensations surging wildly through her body. God, how could this have happened? How could she have *let* it happen? That she was vulnerable was no excuse. She had recognized that fact, along with her own attraction to Morgan McCain. She should have guarded against both—against *him!* Instead, she had permitted him to kiss her—and she had reveled in the potent feelings he had unleashed inside her; she had ached for more. If Morgan had not released her when he had, she had no doubt he would even now be carrying her upstairs to her bedroom to make love to her, or simply flinging her down on the kitchen floor—with her complete and eager compliance!

Despite all her bold talk, how *could* she go to work at the One-Eyed Jacks Oil & Gas Company now? Cat asked herself, distressed. Especially after the way things had turned out with Spence, and with Morgan's obvious feelings about mixing business with pleasure? But then she realized he had undoubtedly hoped his parting words to her *would,* in fact, discourage her from coming into the office tomorrow morning; that if she felt he would be so busy pursuing her personally that he would have no time for her professionally, she would give up the whole idea of becoming a working partner in the corporation.

At that thought, Cat's eyes abruptly narrowed and her temper rose.

"Damn you, Morgan!" she snapped indignantly. "I am *not* going to be dissuaded from trying to fulfill my obligations as a stockholder, from trying to take over Dad's position at One-Eyed Jacks just because *you* don't think I can do the job—much less because you think you can't keep your hands to yourself at the office! Once bitten, twice shy—and I've already learned my lesson the hard way from Spence. We'll be business partners, you and I, Morgan—and that's all we'll be!"

But as she involuntarily remembered the feel of his mouth on her own, tasting her, arousing her unbearably, Cat nevertheless had a terrible, sneaking suspicion this was going to prove much more easily said than done.

Nine

Corporate Politics

The following morning, bright and early, Cat drove to the offices of the One-Eyed Jacks Oil & Gas Company. She did not know what she had expected, but it was not the low, sprawling cluster of glass-and-red-brick buildings that lined the man-made waterway at the grassy edge of the office park. As she walked toward the edifice that housed the One-Eyed Jacks offices, she surveyed her surroundings with approval, noting the trees that had been planted and the other landscaping that had been done. That was one thing Cat had to admit she liked about Wichita: it was green, with trees, bushes, flowers and grass all over. Even the downtown area was beautifully landscaped, it was not just the parks. It *was* pleasant, Cat thought, not to be surrounded by towering blocks of steel and concrete, not to walk in shadow on even the sunniest of days. Away from downtown, there were no skyscrapers to speak of. The building she was now entering was only three stories tall.

The heavy glass door closed behind her with a whisper, shutting out the sounds of the early morning traffic, leaving the interior of the edifice so quiet that Cat felt briefly as though she had entered a library. A short staircase rose from the center of the foyer, and a glance at the directory that hung on one brick wall confirmed that the One-Eyed Jacks Oil & Gas Company was on the second floor. Her mouth was suddenly dry from agitation and her heart thudded with excitement as she slowly climbed the steps to the hallway beyond. It was not just the thought of beginning her new job that filled her with such nervous anticipation, but also the prospect of seeing Morgan again and of his reaction to her presence at the corporation they now owned, if not equally, at least jointly.

Of course he had issued that warning to her yesterday merely to prevent her from showing up at the office this morning. Of course he had. It was foolish to think otherwise, to think that perhaps he had been serious. Of course she was safe alone with him. He had been teasing her, that was all. Still, Cat's pulse raced—because what if he had not been? In that case, how could she trust him—or herself in his presence? she wondered as she remembered his kisses and their potent effect upon her. It was not enough to admit she was vulnerable at the moment, because even if she had not been, the simple truth was she was strongly attracted to Morgan.

Reaching the office doors of the One-Eyed Jacks Oil & Gas Company, Cat paused and drew a deep breath. Then she pushed open the wooden door with its brass lettering and went in. The young receptionist, seated at the desk in the reception area, was obviously expecting her.

"Good morning, Ms. Devlin."

"How . . . how did you know who I was?"

The woman smiled. "Mr. McCain described you very well."

"Indeed?" Cat commented dryly, wondering just *how* he had described her. "Then you probably also know I'll be working here from now on, that I'll be taking my father's place in the business."

"So Mr. McCain has informed us. I'm Josie Kendricks, by the way." The receptionist extended her hand, and Cat shook it firmly. "If you'll follow me, I'll introduce you to Mrs. Whittingdale, who was your father's personal secretary, as well as being Mr. McCain's. She'll show you to your father's office and get you whatever you need."

Despite the perky brunette's engaging friendliness, a puzzled frown knit Cat's brow as she followed the receptionist into a hallway that led to the inner offices of the corporation. Clearly, Morgan had not believed she would heed his warning, but had instead expected her at the One-Eyed Jacks Oil & Gas Company this morning, had even paved the way for her. The mystery was why had he done it? Then, as she remembered their past meetings, a wry smile tugged at the corners of her mouth. No doubt Morgan had thought of her fiery redhead's temper and had sought to avoid any unpleasantness at the corporation. Well, that suited her just fine. She had twice got off on the wrong foot with Morgan. She certainly did not want to do the same with the employees of the One-Eyed Jacks Oil & Gas Company.

"Ms. Devlin, this is Mrs. Whittingdale," Josie announced as they reached the secretary's office, "affectionately known around here as Whitty."

As the older woman rose from her desk, Cat was immediately struck by both the shrewdness and the warmth in her bright, twinkling blue eyes. Gray-haired, plainly but impeccably groomed in a tailored suit, Whitty looked as though she would have been right at home taking tea with the Queen Mum rather than taking dictation. Still, there was a motherly air about her that softened the severity of her appearance and spoke of her kindness. Smiling, sensing she had found not only a friend but also an ally, Cat stretched out her hand, which Whitty shook, then patted in a brisk but caring manner.

"I'll admit I was skeptical at first when Morgan said you were going to take Frank's place here at One-Eyed Jacks," Whitty declared in a no-nonsense fashion. "But now that I've seen you, I can tell there's a good deal of your father in you, Ms. Devlin."

"Cat... please, call me Cat."

"That's a bargain only if you'll agree to call me Whitty in return. Mrs. Whittingdale is too much of a mouthful for anybody!" The secretary chuckled. "My, my... Frank's daughter. Morgan said you were attractive—but then, seeing as how he's said as much about *me* in the past, I didn't pay him a whole lot of mind initially. But now I realize he wasn't exaggerating one iota in his description of you—and from the way he behaved when he talked about you, I have the strangest feeling things are shortly going to get very interesting around here at One-Eyed Jacks, that you're going to liven the place up considerably with your presence. So why don't you come along with me into Frank's office, and we'll have us a cup of coffee and a lovely little chat. Then I'll start showing you some of the ropes of the oil-and-gas business."

"That would be wonderful, Whitty," Cat declared, meaning her words sincerely, for she sensed the secretary, even more than Morgan, could have proved to be a real stumbling block at the corporation, making things very difficult for her indeed. To have Whitty on her side helped tremendously.

Following coffee with the secretary in what had once been Frank Devlin's office, Cat found herself alone at her father's huge antique desk, examining a towering stack of what Whitty had termed oil-and-gas leases. Leafing through them, Cat could not help but shake her head with both amazement and amusement. Some of the documents were so old that they defined the regions covered in the leases in antiquated language she thought could hardly be legal in this day and age. *That area bounded on the north along a line from Farmer Thomas's well to the boulder known as the Black Rock at the edge of the Widow Piper's property* was just one example she read. She discovered that in many cases not just the rights to the property's oil and gas were leased, but also to its minerals. Cat sighed at the realization, because that meant even more to learn. Still, she became so engrossed in reading the documents that the morning fairly flew by, and she was surprised when Morgan, after knocking on the office door, opened it and stuck his head inside.

"You mean you haven't given up yet and gone home in despair?" he said in greeting, his now-familiar, crooked grin curving his mouth so that she knew he was teasing her—even if he *did* wish she'd never come to the offices of the One-Eyed Jacks Oil & Gas Company to begin with.

"Then this horrendous pile of leases filled—at least in several instances—with delightfully archaic legalese was your idea?" She motioned to the stack of papers before her, wishing her pulse had not begun to leap erratically at just the sight of him, that the memory of his kisses yesterday had not risen in her mind.

"No... if you must know, it was Whitty's idea. She said everybody—including me—had had to start somewhere to learn about the oil-and-gas business, and that you might as well begin with the leases."

"Well, they certainly have been very informative. I have to admit that other than as something that makes automobiles go, I hadn't ever really given much thought to gasoline before—where it comes from, how it's discovered, how it's taken from the ground, how it's refined and marketed, et cetera." As she spoke, Cat stood, sliding around the desk to perch on its front edge, having some notion that this would put her more at Morgan's eye level so she would not be disadvantaged by his looking down at her as he strolled into her father's office . . . her office now.

But after a moment, she wished she had stayed where she was, for her new vantage point gave her an excellent view of Morgan—of the slow, sexy, subtle swagger of his hips as he walked toward her. There were so few men who moved with such a combination of power and grace, she thought, fascinated despite herself. It was an inherent trait, not something that could be learned. It made her think of a predator on the prowl, muscles rippling and bunching as the animal prepared to spring. So strong was this impression that Cat instinctively leaned back a little as Morgan came to a halt before her, so she wound up looking up at him anyway, her throat bared in an age-old gesture of submission that made her feel inadvertently exposed and vulnerable. She was vividly conscious of the heat that emanated from Morgan's body, and of how his eyes traveled from the tips of her shoes up her hose-clad legs, lingering on the curve of her breasts beneath the jacket of her lemon yellow linen suit before finally coming to rest on her face.

Ill-concealed desire smoldered in the depths of his ice blue eyes, making them appear perversely like blue flame—clear, pure, brilliant—against the bronze of his skin. At the far corners of his eyes, fine laugh lines etched his visage; deeper grooves bracketed his mustache and mouth. Cat had a sudden, wild urge to reach up and trace the contours of those lines, that mustache, that mouth. She wondered what Morgan would do if she did, if that would prove to be the spark to ignite him. She shuddered faintly at the thought, knowing she was playing with fire and that if she did not want to be burned, she must keep things between them on a strictly businesslike basis.

"What . . . what can I do for you, Morgan?"

"Well, now I believe that if I put my mind to it, I could think of some *very* entertaining answers to that question." He placed one hand on either side of her, on top of the desk, effectively hemming her in so she could not escape. "And it occurs to me that you must want to hear those answers, or you would not have shown up here this morning after my warning to you yesterday."

"Indeed? Then let me disabuse you of that notion," Cat rejoined tartly, heat suffusing her own body despite herself as he leaned over her. "I'm here to do a job, *not* to be seduced! You were right about mixing business with pleasure. I learned that the hard way... with Spence. I thought he and I could be engaged, could even get married and could eventually work together as partners in the import-export firm. But I was wrong—and that's a mistake I don't intend to make again, especially with you! So if your visit to my office is of a personal nature, then I'm afraid I'll have to ask you to leave, *Mr. McCain.*"

He was silent for a long moment, staring down at her. Then he spoke. "What went wrong at the import-export firm? Did you try to take it over, too... to boss Spence around?"

"No, I most certainly did not! But I *did* expect my judgment and decisions to be respected—not to be overruled merely because Spence had the mistaken notion that all women were emotionally unsuited for top-management positions!"

"Well, *I* never said anything like that."

"Didn't you?" Cat snapped, her temper rising—not to mention her temperature at his proximity. "Oh, perhaps not in so many words, but wasn't the message the same?"

"No. As I told you yesterday, I doubt your ability to do the job you've set your mind on, yes—but not because you're a woman. The fact that you're a woman is *my* problem, Cat, because I find you attractive, and you are therefore a distraction. Still, if necessary, I can learn to live with that, I suppose."

"Oh?" She deliberately arched one brow to make her skepticism plain. "Is that why you said I was no longer safe alone with you then?"

"No, I said that in the heat of the moment, just so you'd know that even if you decided to come here to One-Eyed Jacks, it wouldn't necessarily place you off-limits in my mind.... Damn it, Cat! Do you want me to apologize for kissing you yesterday? Is that it?"

She shook her head, because how could she insist on that? Despite Morgan's words, which had seemingly suggested otherwise, she knew he was not the sort of man to force himself on a woman. He would have released her yesterday at any moment she had voiced a protest. Instead, she had remained silent, had reveled in his kisses. How could she insist he apologize, when she was as much to blame as he?

"Yesterday shouldn't have happened." Her voice was softer now. "There are so many reasons why it shouldn't have happened."

"But it *did* happen, Cat." Morgan's own voice was equally low, and underlaid now with a husky note of urgency and desire.

"Yes. But that doesn't mean it has to happen again. Look, Morgan, I'd like for us to be business partners...even friends—"

"But not lovers?" The burning intensity of his gaze scalded her. Tension stretched between them. For a moment Cat was half frightened, half exhilarated by the thought that he meant to kiss her again, such was the passion that darkened his face. But instead, after an instant, with difficulty, Morgan forced a rueful smile to his lips, and when he spoke, his tone was resolutely light. "Now, why did I have the sneaking suspicion you were going to tell me that? Even so, it's not going to work, you know. Feel-

ings—strong feelings—are hard to fight, and I'm not at all
sure I want to battle mine anyway. Still, if you insist, I
suppose I must try." He paused briefly and, to her perverse disappointment, moved a little away from her, as
though he no longer trusted himself to stand so close. Then
he continued. "I came to your office to insist upon taking
you to lunch. However, you mustn't think of it as an actual date, Cat, but, rather, as a . . . power lunch. Isn't that
what, these days, they call what used to be known as a
three-martini lunch?" He smiled once more—an engaging, wicked grin, so she knew that was not how he would
have phrased his invitation only a few minutes ago, before
she had made her position plain. "I thought we could discuss the business and celebrate your becoming a part of
One-Eyed Jacks."

If she had any sense at all, Cat knew she should refuse.
After all, she had already laid out the ground rules of their
relationship, and she had to adhere to them or Morgan
would not take her seriously, about either him or her job at
the corporation.

"All right," she heard herself reply instead. "A power
lunch it is then."

Cat was astounded by her own response. She must be out
of her mind, she thought, dismayed. But then she rea-
soned that there was nothing wrong with having lunch with
a colleague, and she and Morgan really *did* have business
to discuss. So what if he had admitted that he was attracted to her, if the way he glanced at her was anything but
businesslike? So what if she could not seem to put his kisses
from her mind, if every time she looked at him, she wished
he would kiss her again? Her breath caught in her throat at
the realization. She was being foolish, behaving like some
high school girl with a silly crush. She simply had to get
hold of herself and her emotions.

Sliding from the edge of the desk, she grabbed her
handbag and drew its long leather strap over her shoulder.

"Perhaps Whitty would like to join us," she suggested. "After meeting her this morning, I'm sure she knows almost as much as you—if not more—about One-Eyed Jacks and the oil-and-gas business."

"No doubt." Morgan's tone was dry. "But actually, I hadn't planned on making this a threesome. However, if you don't trust yourself alone with me, if you feel you need a chaperon, Cat . . ."

"Certainly not!" she retorted, flushing, because of course that was precisely why she had suggested asking Whitty to join them.

"Then let's go, shall we?" Taking Cat's arm, he ushered her from the office. "Whitty," he said to the secretary as they passed her desk, "Cat and I will be having lunch at Applebee's if you need us."

"All right, Morgan. You kids have fun," Whitty replied.

"We've . . . got a lot of business to go over." Cat could feel another blush creeping up her cheeks at the knowing twinkle in the secretary's eyes.

"Of course," Whitty agreed, positively beaming.

"Do you know what she thinks?" Cat hissed, mortified, once they were outside in the parking lot and climbing into Morgan's Bronco.

"Yes. She has been trying to marry me off for years, ever since she started to work at One-Eyed Jacks, in fact." He shook his head ruefully, chuckling. "She thinks I need to give up my wild, wicked ways and settle down. So far her endeavors to procure me a bride have proved unsuccessful—much to her despair. However, as you will come to learn, once Whitty has her mind set on something, she's like a feisty terrier with an old bone—she doesn't let go easily. Rather like you, I should imagine."

Cat had the good grace to laugh at that. "Yes, I'll confess that persistence has always been one of my strong suits.

Have you never even come close to marriage then, Morgan?'' she inquired curiously.

For a moment she thought he wasn't going to answer her. His lighthearted mood abruptly dissipated, and with more force than was necessary, he jammed the key into the ignition of the Bronco, starting the engine up with a roar. "One near miss,'' he finally announced tersely, a muscle flexing in his jaw, so Cat knew without even asking that he spoke of the woman he had on a previous occasion said he would prefer to forget, the one of whom she, Cat, had reminded him. "We were engaged, but it . . . didn't work out.''

Cat felt her resemblance to his lost love must be hard for Morgan. At least he did not make her think of Spence. . . . No, now that she thought about it, that was not quite true. In some ways, he *had* reminded her of Spence. Of course most people did have a particular physical type to whom they were attracted. There were some men who preferred blondes, for example; others who were drawn only to brunettes. Cat herself had always liked tall, dark men. Such as Spence and Morgan.

"Was she a redhead, your fiancée?''

"No, a blonde . . . but the kind who knew Bach from Beethoven—and old money from new. In the end she decided she preferred the former.''

Cat detected a note of bitterness in Morgan's voice, and she knew the breakup had hurt him more than he would ever admit, such was his pride.

"Ouch,'' she said lightly. "Sounds like your blonde and Spence would have made a go of it. He was . . . something of a snob, too, I'm afraid.''

"And you're not?''

"No . . . no, I don't think I am—at least, I hope I'm not. I never wanted to be my mother, you see . . . someone who would throw away a chance at love, at happiness, because the man was poor or lacked social position or whatever. I loved my father, Morgan, no matter what his failings might have been. He was a fine man. The more I knew him, the more I came to understand that. I was proud to be his daughter. I was . . . I *am* proud of what he accomplished in his life. Nobody ever handed him anything on a plate. He started with nothing, and together with you, he built One-Eyed Jacks. That's why I'm so determined to learn all I can about the oil-and-gas business, why I plan on succeeding at this job—with or without your help and regardless of your personal feelings or mine.''

"All right. That seems fair enough,'' Morgan replied as he pulled into Applebee's parking lot and killed the Bronco's engine. "Why don't we just agree to play things by ear then and see where they go from here?''

"That sounds good.''

They went inside the restaurant, which was crowded. Fortunately, Whitty had foreseen this and had prudently phoned ahead for reservations. So after Morgan gave his name to the hostess, they were seated at a table fairly quickly. After glancing at the menu, Cat ordered the Santa Fe chicken salad, while Morgan decided on the Applebee's steak dinner. Then, much to her surprise, he took his Waterman fountain pen from his shirt pocket and, on the back of a napkin, began to draw a diagram that demonstrated the basics of drilling an oil well.

"I think it'd make explaining this a little easier if you'd move around here and sit beside me, Cat, so we can both see what I'm doodling—since, admittedly, I'm no artist." He indicated the chair next to him.

She glanced at him suspiciously for some sign that he was flirting with her, testing her resolve not to become involved with him, but she could read nothing of his thoughts. He was wearing what she had come to recognize as his poker face. Still, she *did* want to learn, so after a minute Cat moved around the table to take the chair beside him. Bending her head to study the diagram he had drawn, she missed the smile that curved Morgan's mouth beneath his mustache before he began to tell her all about how to dig black gold from the earth.

Ten

The Play's the Thing

In the weeks that followed, Cat applied herself diligently to learning everything she could about the oil-and-gas industry. She made several trips downtown to the main library to check out books, which she lugged home to read and study at night. During the day, she continued her work at the offices of the One-Eyed Jacks Oil & Gas Company, and although she had as yet to make any real decisions there, she grew more confident in her knowledge as time wore on. She had discovered that in addition to its offices, the corporation had a building at a second location, a corrugated steel structure that resembled a large garage or a small plant, where vehicles, machinery, equipment, parts and other supplies were stored and out of which the pumpers and other employees who handled the actual day-to-day, hands-on operations and on-site labor worked. The main offices were referred to at the company as "HQ," for headquarters, and the second building, managed by a foreman, was called simply "the shop."

Much to Cat's surprise, for she had fully expected Morgan to fight her every hard-won step of the way, he instead treated her like a management trainee, making certain her education about the oil-and-gas business was as thorough as possible. He took her out to the shop to show her what went on there. Although a receptionist-secretary worked in a cubbyhole of an office at the back, the shop was clearly a man's milieu. Its green-glassed windows, barricaded with chicken wire and lined with taped alarm wire as a precaution against break-ins, were cracked in places and coated so thickly with grime that it was almost impossible to see through them. The concrete floors were stained with blotches of oil and grease. Next to the time clock hung a giant bulletin board boasting, among other things, a pin-up-girl calendar and a couple of risqué French postcards. Beneath was a long metal table on which sat message bins, untidy piles of dusty brochures and coffee-stained papers, and an ashtray filled to overflowing. In the men's small bathroom, the door of which stood open, Cat spied a stack of *Playboy* magazines on the floor in one corner.

"Good heavens, this place is a pigsty! Why haven't you done something about cleaning it up?" Cat asked Morgan, frowning at him with disapproval.

"Now, darlin', do try to keep that temper of yours under control," he drawled, grinning at her. "Because the one thing you're not going to change at One-Eyed Jacks is the shop, believe me. You could straighten this place up and fix it up as fancy as you pleased and a week later it'd look just like this again. It's mostly men who work here—and the majority of 'em have blue-collar backgrounds and a high school education, if that. Not that I'm knocking 'em, mind. For the most part, they're decent, hardworking men, and I trust 'em to take care of what I need taken care of. But yuppies they just aren't, babe."

"Don't call me that—or 'darlin'' or any other name of that ilk! It's sexist and demeaning in a professional environment!" Cat snapped. "And so are that...that calendar, those postcards, and those magazines! I want them, at least, removed from the premises immediately!"

"The men'd just bring 'em back tomorrow, Cat," Morgan stated matter-of-factly, no longer smiling. "And I reckon you must have thought Frank was pretty 'sexist and demeaning,' too—since he called all the gals at the office, including Whitty, 'sugar.'"

Cat was nonplussed by this discovery. "He—he did?"

"Yeah, he did. On the other hand, the few women who work the wells and pipelines are paid the exact same wages as their male counterparts at One-Eyed Jacks." He pointed to the Equal Employment Opportunity sign encased in glass and hanging prominently on one wall. "Frank believed in that, as do I. And it's true what they say, you know—actions *do* speak louder than words."

"Is that...is that why you're helping me, training me?" she queried curiously.

"Yes. I still don't know whether you'll prove able to take Frank's place at One-Eyed Jacks, Cat. But you were hell-bent-for-leather determined to try, and it wouldn't be right of me not to give you that chance. Besides which, I want you to know that if you wind up blowing it, it for damned sure won't be because you're a woman and because I, a man, stood in your way! It'll be for the simple reason that you just couldn't cut the mustard, Cat—and you won't have anybody but your own sweet self to blame for that!"

She was so astounded by Morgan's words that for a moment she could only stare at him, speechless. Then, at last, she spoke. "I suppose I should thank you for that."

"Yes, you should," he insisted dryly.

"Well, then...thank you."

"You're welcome. Now, can we get out of here and leave the shop in peace? Or do you make it a general policy to give every man you meet a hard time?"

With difficulty, Cat bit back the retort that sprang to her lips. Deep down inside, she knew Morgan was right, that the minute her back was turned, the pin-up-girl calendar and the French postcards would be tacked back onto the bulletin board and the *Playboy* magazines returned to the men's rest room. It was, as Morgan had once told her, simply the nature of the beast. She sighed, shaking her head.

"Fine! But I'm sending a Fabio calendar down here today—and the next time I come here, I expect to see it hanging right up there beside the Vargas Girl!"

Morgan threw back his head and laughed uproariously at that. "Oh, Cat, you're a woman after my own heart, I do believe!"

Together, they exited the shop—much, she felt sure, to the relief of the foreman and his men. After that, Morgan drove her out to tour some of the sites she had read about in the oil-and-gas leases that first day at the company. As she and Morgan rode along, Cat observed herds of cattle and sheep grazing in fields bounded by barbed wire and farmers driving big combines, in the process of harvesting acres of golden wheat. Here and there some of the fields already cleared were being burned. The windows of the Bronco were down, and on the wind that streamed into the vehicle, she smelled the pungent scent of what she thought was marijuana.

"My God, that's pot burning!" she exclaimed, startled.

"That's sure what it smells like, isn't it?" Morgan agreed affably. "And out here in the country, it's certainly a possibility. Sometimes the ranchers and farmers don't even know it's being grown on their land—particularly more-isolated sections—courtesy of would-be drug dealers. However, more than likely it's just what's left of plain old alfalfa that's already been cut. When it burns, it smells just like grass going up in smoke.''

They had by now reached some of the oil-well sites, and Morgan turned off onto a narrow dirt path, then parked the Bronco. After they got out of the vehicle and began to walk across the field, he indicated the beam pump that was their goal.

"That's Three of a Kind Number One, and that one over there—'' he pointed to another beam pump in the distance ''—is Three of a Kind Number Two. Unless a landowner voices some stringent objection, One-Eyed Jacks has a policy of naming its wells after poker hands and cards in general.''

"And when the landowner objects?''

"Then we usually wind up calling the well after the landowner...Hank Souther Number One, for instance. All the wells have both names and numbers. That's how we keep them straight. After we choose a name for a lease site, all the wells at that location are numbered in the order they're drilled. So the wells here on Mrs. Williams's property, for example, are named Three of a Kind and numbered one through four, since we have four wells here.''

"The beam pumps are so ugly in reality, compared to the diagrams I've seen,'' Cat declared as she studied Three of Kind Number One more closely.

"Yeah, these are older wells. Nowadays, since the world's become more conscious of its environment and ecology, we try harder not to disturb the surrounding land so much, to work more in harmony with nature.'' He went on to explain to her how a well was drilled and machinery operated, the way in which the natural gas was siphoned off and a dozen other things that made her recognize just how vast Morgan's knowledge was, especially compared to her own.

Later on, however, when, in the weeks that passed, he took her to visit one of the local oil refineries to which the

One-Eyed Jacks Oil & Gas Company marketed its crude oil,
Cat did not feel nearly so ignorant. The principles of mar-
keting she understood backward and forward. A few days
after that, she confidently entered Morgan's office to inform him that according to her research, One-Eyed Jacks
could make more money by selling its crude to a different
refinery.

"Yes, I know," he said.

"Then...I don't understand. We *are* in business to make
a profit, aren't we? So why aren't we selling our crude to
that refinery?" Cat asked, genuinely puzzled.

"For the simple reason that I refuse to do business with
any refinery that dumps toxic waste into the environment,
darlin'."

"Do you know for a fact that that particular refinery
does that?"

"I do."

"Then why haven't you done anything about it, reported it to the proper authorities?"

"There isn't any need to, that's why. That refinery is under investigation even as we speak. But like those of jus-
tice, the wheels of government bureaucracy grind slowly.
It'll be years before all the facts are uncovered, a decision
is reached and that refinery is fined, forced to clean up its
act, and the heads of its management roll. Until that time,
however, One-Eyed Jacks' crude goes elsewhere—or do you
still want to question that?" Morgan raised one eyebrow
inquiringly.

"No, I don't."

"Good. Now, what are your plans for this weekend?"

The abrupt change of topic momentarily threw Cat off
stride.

"This—this weekend?" she parroted lamely.

"Yes, I have season tickets to Music Theater, and I
thought you might like to accompany me to Friday night's
performance." Morgan grinned when Cat, torn by her

conflicting emotions, hesitated. "You needn't think of it as an actual socks-on car date, Cat," he declared.

"A socks-on car date? What in the hell is that?"

"Just what it sounds like—a date that requires a man to wear socks with his shoes and to pick his date up in a car."

"As opposed to what, for heaven's sake?"

"As opposed to his throwing a pair of sneakers on his bare feet right before she drives herself over to his house, bringing the beer and pizza with her."

"That's not a date," Cat asserted, disgusted. "That's a delivery service!"

"Only if she delivers," Morgan rejoined, impudently waggling his eyebrows à la Groucho Marx and tapping an imaginary cigar as he spoke, then grinning even more widely at the blush that stained Cat's cheeks crimson.

"Don't you dare ask me if *I* deliver, Morgan McCain!" she warned, doing her best to repress the answering smile that tugged at her lips in response to his antics.

"How *did* you guess that was going to be my next question? Never mind. Don't answer that. You'll only say something insulting about my dubious character—and then I'll be forced to admit it's probably true. Now, about Music Theater..." He determinedly returned to their previous topic of conversation. "Before you decline my invitation, I feel compelled to point out that it is one of *the* places to see and be seen in Wichita. And although I don't give a damn about that—and I'm beginning pleasantly to suspect you don't, either—it *will* offer you a prime opportunity to meet many of this town's movers and shakers, several of whom One-Eyed Jacks does business with. Therefore, if it suits you to do so, you may legitimately think of it as a professional social occasion—and not a real date with me at all," he ended blandly, his thick, spiky black lashes hooding his eyes, so she could not tell what he was thinking at that moment.

Despite her resolve not to get involved in a relationship with Morgan that was other than professional, Cat found herself wanting badly to accept his invitation. Both to her dismay and to her provocation, she had discovered that the more time she spent with him, the more she learned about him, the better she knew him, the more strongly attracted to him she had become. Deep down inside, she knew that if she were honest with herself, she must admit she had already halfway fallen in love with him. He was not only the most ruggedly handsome man she had ever seen, but also intelligent, honest, ethical, compassionate and appealingly down-to-earth. That he was also wild and wicked merely added spice to the mixture.

"What's playing at Music Theater?" she finally asked, telling herself sternly that she would be a fool to turn down an opportunity to mingle with those who belonged to what she had learned was commonly and sometimes scornfully referred to as Wichita's "21 Club." "Something like *Annie, Get Your Gun,* no doubt."

"No, actually, it's *Cabaret.*"

Of course it had to be one of her all-time favorites—slick and witty, socially provocative and insightful.

"All right. I'll go with you," Cat said. "What should I wear?"

"The same thing you'd wear to a performance on Broadway."

"And just how would you know what anybody wears to the theater in New York, Morgan?"

"Just because I choose to live in Wichita doesn't mean I haven't been to the Big Apple, darlin'—several times, in fact. It's a great place to visit . . . lots of fun and exciting things to do. It's a habit of mine to go there every so often, generally on my way to Europe. I even went with Frank once or twice—although, I'm forced to confess, I foolishly declined the pleasure of making your acquaintance then, having the horribly mistaken notion that you and I wouldn't exactly hit it off. Last time I saw both *Phantom of the Opera* and *Les Miserables*. And that's how I know what's worn to the theater in New York.''

''I see. So you're not quite the simple cowboy you sometimes appear. That being the case, may I then safely assume you will *not* be attired in a Stetson hat, Levi's jeans and Tony Lama boots when you pick me up Friday night?'' Cat queried archly.

''You may.''

Nor was he when, at the appointed hour on Friday evening, he arrived to pick her up. In fact, after opening her front door to admit him, Cat could only stand and stare, her breath catching in her throat. From his stylish, European-cut, black Armani suit to the traditional Cole Haans on his feet, Morgan looked not as though he'd stepped from a Marlboro cigarette advertisement, but from the glossy pages of *GQ*. Spence at his best had nothing on Morgan.

''Unless you're waiting for me to kiss you, close your mouth, Cat,'' he said in greeting, grinning at her obvious astonishment. ''Because you look so damned gorgeous that I'm sorely tempted to sample a taste of you!''

Cat blushed at both his compliment and the suggestion that he might kiss her—even though she knew with certainty she had seldom looked better. She had taken inordinate care with her appearance, trying on first one dress and then another before she had finally settled on her ''little black dress,'' which was a basic but dramatic, clinging silk sheath with a halter strap and no back. She had left her dark red hair loose and flowing, and the contrast of it and her pale skin with the dress was vivid. Her jewelry was simple but equally sensational—a pair of dangling gold earrings and a single, heavy gold bangle bracelet on her right wrist.

''Let me just get my handbag and wrap,'' she told him. ''Then we'll go.'' Once outside, she paused momentarily at the sight of the sleek black Corvette parked in the half-circle drive. "Is this yours?" She motioned toward the sports car.

"Yeah . . . a '68 that I rebuilt and restored myself. I got it out of my garage earlier this evening. Somehow I had a sneaking suspicion that I'd be taking a long, cool woman in a black dress to the theater, and the Bronco just didn't seem to fit the occasion." He opened the Corvette's passenger door for her. "Get in."

Music Theater was held at the Century II's Concert Hall, Morgan informed her during their drive to the downtown area, and the performance of *Cabaret* was sold out. After he had parked the sports car in the circular building's huge parking lot, they strolled toward the edifice itself and up its gently inclined steps. Inside, Cat saw that the continuous, curved hallway that encompassed the interior did double duty by serving as an art gallery. Paintings hung all along the walls, small, discreet white price cards tucked into the right-hand corner of each frame. Greeting people he knew, Morgan ushered Cat into the theater, where she discovered that they had excellent seats front and center. The orchestra was just in the process of tuning up. Drawing off her lacy shawl, then settling into her chair, she leafed through her program, pretending not to notice when Morgan slid his arm along the top of her seat back, lightly brushing her bare shoulders. Still, the sensation was so erotic—especially after the house lights had dimmed—that she could hardly concentrate on the show.

His touch was like fire against her skin, igniting an answering spark in her as she listened to the music she knew by heart. The fact that all through the first half of the performance, Morgan played idly with her hair and caressed her shoulder languidly did not help. It only fanned the initial spark to flame, so that by the time that intermission rolled around and the house lights came up, she felt as though she were burning up with fever. Instead of watching Sally Bowles's plight on stage, Cat had kept drifting away into one fantasy after another—each of which had ended with Morgan making love to her. Prompted by the musical, she had even envisioned herself as a cabaret singer and stuck Morgan in a military uniform! Now she could hardly look at him as he escorted her into the lobby and asked her whether she wanted any refreshments.

"There's no alcohol served here, of course. But I can get you a soft drink and a candy bar if you'd like," he told her.

"A—a cola would be fine," she replied, glad of an excuse to get rid of him for a few minutes until she could force her thoughts into a more orderly channel. Besides, maybe a soft drink would cool her down!

Still, as she watched him stroll over to the refreshment bar, she could not help but admire him. He was undoubtedly the most handsome man present tonight, she thought, noticing—not without a violent twinge of jealousy—how many women eyed him appraisingly and flirted with him invitingly as he made his way through the crowd, pausing now and then to shake hands with various men. When he finally returned, he handed Cat her cola, then proceeded to point out who was who in Wichita, introducing her to several prominent, influential people.

"Why, as I live and breathe, I do believe it's Morgan McCain! You handsome outlaw, you! What in the world are you doing here? Music Theater's not generally *your* particular brand of home brew," a tall, cool blonde drawled as she approached them, towing behind her a man Cat knew intuitively came from generations of old money.

She did not need to hear Morgan greet the woman to know this was his ex-fiancée, Veronica Havers—the whole story of whom Whitty had told her at the office. Now, seeing Veronica, Cat recognized the type instantly. She had seen a hundred Veronicas before at her mother's parties and wherever else social predators were to be found, prowling in their sleek attire and baring their sharp claws. Cat disliked Veronica on sight, and she knew the feeling was mutual.

"Ronnie," Morgan said coolly, then nodded to the man. "Paul."

"Aren't you going to introduce us to your...friend, Morgan?" Veronica prodded.

"Yes, of course. Cat, these are the Stirlings...Ronnie and Paul. And this is Frank Devlin's daughter, Cat. I'm sure you probably heard about Frank's death."

"Yes, such an unexpected tragedy...a heart attack, wasn't it? Our sympathies on your loss, Ms. Devlin." Veronica surveyed Cat assessingly, mentally toting up the cost of her dress, jewelry, shoes and handbag—a process that was not lost on Cat.

It was one of those rare occasions when she was actually grateful to her mother for being such a snob. Because of Julia Talbot, Cat knew how to deal with women who wielded words and glances like the keenest of daggers.

"Thank you, Ms. Stirling. It's very kind of you to say so."

"Cat's down from New York," Morgan explained. "She's taken Frank's place at One-Eyed Jacks. Her extensive experience in importing and exporting coupled with her background in both the European and Asian business markets are giving the company a fresh and exciting perspective."

"I'm sure that Ms. Devlin has indeed proved a valuable asset—in more ways than one. How...nice for you, Morgan." Clearly, Veronica was in reality insinuating how wonderful it was that Morgan now had a partner with whom he could sleep—*and* keep the stock all in the family, so to speak.

At Veronica's words, Cat could feel her blood pressure skyrocketing. "Actually, Ms. Stirling," she purred in Julia Talbot's best cat fashion, laying her hand lightly on Morgan's arm and gazing up at him seductively before flashing Veronica a brilliant smile, "it's very nice for both of us, isn't it, Morgan?"

His eyes danced with knowing amusement and at the same time smoldered with heat as he glanced down at her. He slipped his arm possessively about her waist and drew her up next to him so her head rested on his shoulder.

"It's better than nice, darlin'," he declared huskily, effectively wiping the tight smile off of Veronica's face. "Much better."

To Cat's relief, the lobby lights flashed on and off then, signaling that intermission was coming to an end, so there was no time for further conversation. Morgan made their goodbyes, then led her away, his arm still clasped around her waist, his head bent near to hers as he whispered in her ear.

"Now *that* was a performance worth the price of admission!" He laughed softly. "Hell! Even *I* half believed we're sleeping together! Ronnie's smile disappeared so fast that she looked like she'd accidentally sucked on an unripe persimmon!"

"You don't agree then that *Cabaret* is worth whatever you paid for the tickets?" Cat asked, pointedly ignoring his latter remarks. "If I recall correctly, Ms. Stirling *did* suggest Music Theater wasn't your particular brand of home brew." She knew instinctively that Veronica was watching them walk away together. Cat could practically feel the daggers aimed at her bare back.

"To the contrary, babe," Morgan insisted, his arm tightening about her in a way that sent a sudden rush of heat and excitement through her. "I can't remember when I've enjoyed a musical more."

Cat felt the same, but she was damned if she was going to admit that to Morgan.

"Why? Do you keep a black leather coat and a pair of jackboots hidden in your closet?" Her double entendre was, on the one hand, a reference to the show's World War II setting and the military uniforms of its German officers.

"Naw . . . just a lariat for roping high-strung fillies who chafe at being cut out of the herd and branded."

For the life of her, Cat could not think of a satisfactory comeback to that.

Eleven

Dances and Dreams

The third time Cat noticed the battered old pickup truck in the parking lot of the One-Eyed Jacks office park, it belatedly occurred to her it was the same truck she had seen in Vickridge on the morning following her arrival in Wichita. She had, in fact, observed it in the neighborhood on several occasions since. As she walked toward the glass-and-red-brick building, now so familiar that it felt like a second home to her, her brow was knit in a puzzled frown. It was entirely possible, she supposed, that the vehicle *did*, in fact, belong to a lawn service that not only mowed yards in Vickridge, but also cared for the landscaping at the office park. But for the first time this morning, she realized that in all the times she had seen the pickup, she had *not* viewed any lawn mowers in its bed or in use in the vicinity. At the very least, the situation was certainly odd. It made her feel anxious now, as though perhaps someone were spying on her. Maybe she should mention it to Morgan, Cat mused. But then she remembered what had happened when she had mistaken *him* for a stalker, and she told herself her uneasiness about the truck was due to nothing more than her imagination working overtime again. In fact, the more she dwelled upon it, the thought that some lone assailant had singled her out almost upon her very arrival in Wichita seemed highly improbable, even downright fantastic.

Shaking her head and shrugging, she dismissed the notion, forcing herself to concentrate instead on the work that lay ahead of her today. Morgan had given her a number of reports to study, after which he planned to ask her what, if any, wells she would recommend shutting down and why. While she did not mind these tasks he set her—in fact, she enjoyed the challenge tremendously—the manner in which he insisted on conducting his "quizzes," as he called them, had proved both discomfiting and exciting. She could not think of it as other than outrageous blackmail, because he was, in effect, talking her into dates in exchange for his teaching her about the oil-and-gas business. Further, she knew learning how to do her job was only half the reason why she continued to prove such a willing victim.

One afternoon he had told her the day's quiz would take place at the Boat House downtown, a replica of the original Riverside Boat House of Wichita's earlier era. There he had proceeded to rent a canoe, in which he had then paddled the two of them leisurely and romantically down the Big Arkansas river—while interrogating her about how much natural gas wells pumping various amounts of barrels of oil per day should be producing. He had interspersed his questions with remarks about how her eyes were greener than the leaves of the trees lining the river and how, in the sundress and hat she had worn to work that day, she looked, reclining in the bow of the canoe, as though she had just stepped from some Victorian painting.

Another day he had taken her to a stables, where he had hired two horses for them to ride, Western style, despite the fact that Cat had always ridden English. Along a secluded bridle path he had tested her knowledge about the mechanics of beam pumps—while telling her how the sunlight slanting through the limbs of the trees turned her dark red hair to flame and made her skin glow with the luster of a pearl. At the end of the trail, he had leaned over from atop his horse and, taking Cat by surprise, had kissed her lingeringly on the mouth, nearly causing them both to be unseated from their saddles when her mare had started, stamping and switching its tail.

From the windows of the Petroleum Club in the Fourth Financial Center, Cat had watched the flaming orange sun go down over the city, raining fire in the sky. She had played tennis at Riverside Park and racquetball at the Racquet Club. She had ridden the old wooden roller coaster at Joyland, exhilarated by the coveted last car's skipping on the tracks. She had batted baseballs in the batting cages and putted golf balls on the miniature golf course at Sports World. From the Farm and Art Market, she had carried home fresh fruits and vegetables, Indian jewelry and local artwork. In Towanda, a small town not far away, she had bought a carousel horse at Two Lions Antiques and had dined at the Blue Moon Saloon. She had gunned down monsters on the arcade machines at Aladdin's Castle and shot up targets at the Bullseye! Indoor Shooting Range. For a $3.00 ticket that Morgan had insisted on buying, she had actually ridden an elephant at the Shrine Circus and for a quarter, she had bought a bag of popcorn to feed the animals at the Sedgwick County Zoo, famous nationwide for its natural habitats. She had won $500 on a trifecta bet at the Greyhound Park Racetrack and had seen a famous rock group perform at the Kansas Coliseum. In Morgan's Piper Cub plane, she had flown to the little Kansas town of Beaumont for lunch at the Beaumont Hotel. She had discovered that the sleek speedboat stored in her father's garage actually belonged to Morgan when he had driven her out to Lake Afton for a cookout and water skiing. Several of his friends had joined them, and while Cat and the other women sunned themselves on the beach, Morgan and the other men, shouting and laughing, had steered the speedboat so close to shore that the women had been sprayed unmercifully by the speedboat's rooster tail, the giant plume of water it spewed behind it. As a result of his antics, Morgan had received a stern warning from the shore patrol.

Although she had on these occasions acquired a good deal of knowledge about the oil-and-gas industry and, with flying colors, passed all her so-called quizzes, Cat knew she was in reality being cleverly seduced. Worse, all the reasons she kept telling herself why she ought not to embark upon an affair with Morgan appeared increasingly lame whenever she thought about them, mere excuses to hide the real truth: she had fallen in love with him, and she was afraid of being hurt again.

Yet, as though he instinctively sensed as much, Morgan did not press her, rarely did more than kiss her. How he held himself in check, Cat did not know—although she suspected he took numerous long, cold showers. To the best of her knowledge, he saw no other women. Nor did she see any other men, although several she had met had called to ask her out, the other "outlaws" in the rowdy crowd Morgan ran with apparently having no scruples about cutting into one another's time if they could. Cat had turned them all down, and she thought Morgan knew both that they had called her and that she had rejected their invitations, although he never mentioned it to her.

Sighing, she tossed the report she had been reading onto her desk, the figures making little or no sense, since she kept drifting off into reverie, thinking about Morgan. Moments later, as though her thoughts had somehow communicated themselves to him, he knocked on her door, then entered her office.

"Are you free for supper Friday night?" he asked.

"*This* Friday?" She groaned at the prospect, rolling her eyes with disbelief. "Morgan, you have simply *got* to be kidding! There's no way I can be ready for one of your damned quizzes this Friday! You only gave me this stuff two days ago!" She indicated the papers scattered over her desk.

"Well . . . to tell you the truth, Cat, I was thinking we might forget the quiz this time and have an actual socks-on car date for a change. What do you say?"

She said nothing for a long moment—for she knew that, with his words, he was in reality telling her he was tired of playing games, that he wanted to do more than just kiss her good-night at her front door.

"I—I don't know, Morgan—"

"Come on, Cat. You've seen for yourself I don't bite." Wisely, he did not add aloud what he was thinking: that if he had to take one more long, cold shower, he was certain he was going to collapse from hypothermia. "Except that there won't be any quiz, I promise you it won't be different from any of the other times we've gone out—unless you want it to be." He groaned inwardly at the thought that she would not.

"Oh . . . all right then," she finally agreed, knowing that to refuse just because he was not planning on quizzing her would be ridiculously hypocritical.

"Great. I'll pick you up at seven. Wear your jeans and your dancing shoes."

After Morgan had gone, Cat sat staring out her office windows at the winding waterway beyond and thinking she had no sense at all, that she was surely on the road to ruin since she hadn't learned not to make the same mistake twice. Her heart was beating so fast that she wondered if she ought to drive herself to the nearby Minor Emergency

Center and insist on having an EKG run—especially since her father had dropped dead of a heart attack. But deep down inside, she knew she was being silly, that there was nothing wrong with her heart except that she had foolishly given it away to Morgan, even if he did not know it yet. Its speed was due solely to the thought of surrendering her body to him as well, of making love with him.

"Cat, you're a damned fool," she told herself aloud—both then and later, right before she opened her front door to admit him at the agreed-upon hour.

They ate supper in Old Town, at the River City Brewery, a quiet, charming restaurant Cat found both pleasant and entertaining. The interior was all done in highly polished woods, and behind the elegant bar that ran nearly the length of the south wall were not mirrors, but windows, behind which stood the huge, gleaming vats in which the restaurant's own beer was brewed right on the premises. There were several varieties, with different beers offered on different days, so for starters, Morgan insisted on ordering the samples, which came in containers only slightly bigger than shot glasses. Cat tasted them all before finally settling on the Old Town Brown, a delicious dark beer.

"An excellent choice—since that happens to be my own personal favorite, too," Morgan declared as he laid aside his menu. "You have a very discerning palate, Cat."

"For beer, anyway. I'm still not sure about my taste in men, however. I can't believe I allowed you to talk me into an actual 'socks-on car date,' as you insist upon calling it!"

"Did it ever occur to you that maybe it's because you're as weak willed as I am when it comes to fighting the attraction between us? That it's strong enough to have overpowered whatever common sense or scruples we might both possess? No, don't answer that, because I know you're only going to deny it—and that, I won't permit. What I've suggested is no less than the truth, and deep down inside, you know it, Cat."

"Do I?"

"Yes, you do. You're just too proud and stubborn to admit it! I believe that just because of what happened between you and Spencer Kingsley, you've got the mistaken notion that we can't be both business partners and lovers—a notion I'll admit that I shared at first. But I was wrong, just as you are. Our circumstances are different. You don't work for me and I'm not looking at cutting you in on my assets, as Spencer was. You're already a co-owner of One-Eyed Jacks, and I've come to respect your judgment besides. In fact, I'm sorry I initially doubted your ability to do the job. In the weeks you've been at the company, you've learned more about the oil-and-gas business than I thought was possible, and we've worked well together, Cat, you and I. To think we, as two mature adults, can't carry that relationship over into our private lives is foolish. We can. We will."

"Indeed?" Her tone was dry, and she lifted one brow. "Well, isn't that the height of arrogance? You're pretty damned sure of yourself, Morgan. You're pretty damned sure of me!"

"That's because I'm not Spencer, Cat—and you're not Ronnie. And this isn't something that's happening because we're both on the rebound or tied together by Frank or One-Eyed Jacks, either. It's happening because it was meant to, because the chemistry's not just right, it's damned near explosive between us. You feel it, too, Cat. Every time I look at you, kiss you, I can see in your eyes that you do. You want to make love with me just as badly as I want to make love with you."

She did not answer—for the simple reason that she *had* no answer. In her heart of hearts, she knew everything Morgan had said was true. She did not want to go on fighting him, fighting herself and the feelings he stirred so strongly within her. She wanted to go to bed with him, to feel him lying naked beside her in the darkness, to know him intimately, to awaken in the morning and see his head on the pillow next to her own. She was glad that, just then, the waitress appeared with their supper, so their conversation naturally came to a halt while their plates were placed before them.

"Can I get you anything else?" the woman asked.

"Cat?" Morgan glanced at her inquiringly. She shook her head. "No, thank you. That'll be all at the moment," he told the waitress, who smiled and nodded before leaving them alone again.

To Cat's relief, Morgan did not continue their previous discussion, but talked desultorily of this and that, entertaining her with his seemingly endless supply of lighthearted anecdotes, which never failed to amuse her, to make her laugh. That was one of the things that drew her to him, she recognized slowly now—his ability to make her laugh, to make her feel as though she had not a care in the world. It was perhaps that, more than anything, that had helped her through the worst of her initial grief at her father's death, that had made her work at One-Eyed Jacks not just a challenge, but also a pure delight. It occurred to her suddenly how little she had laughed with Spence, how little true pleasure he had taken in the simple things life had to offer. She remembered how, once, when passing by Central Park, she had badgered him into hiring a hansom cab to take them for a drive. No sooner had they got settled in the carriage than, much to her anger and disappointment, Spence had opened up his briefcase and proceeded to use the time to go over some contracts. But Morgan always left his briefcase in the Bronco, and he had devoted his entire attention to her during their trolley ride one afternoon, whispering silly sweet talk in her ear, making her laugh and blush.

Lost in reverie, Cat finished her supper. Then, once Morgan had taken care of the check, they strolled outside beneath the old-fashioned streetlights that lit up the whole of Old Town. Since it was Friday night, the security guards that regularly patrolled the district were out in full force, ensuring that even unescorted females were safe, could park their cars and walk from place to place, if they so chose. There was something for just about everyone in Old Town, Morgan told her, pointing out, among other attractions, the Texas Roadhouse, where live bands entertained Generation X-ers; Heroes, which catered to college jocks, cheerleaders, frat rats and sorority sisters; and the Cowboy.

"That last one's self-explanatory." He grinned.

"And that's where we're going now, I take it."

"Yes, indeed. If you don't already know how, tonight you're going to learn how to dance the cotton-eyed Joe and the two-step."

"Am I?"

"Yes, you are—so don't give me any argument about it."

"Would it surprise you to learn I wasn't planning to—" Cat broke off abruptly, having suddenly spied a battered old pickup truck in one of the parking lots. She was certain the vehicle was the same one she had seen both in Vickridge and outside the offices of the One-Eyed Jacks Oil & Gas Company. She grabbed Morgan's arm, pulling him to a halt. "Do you see that beat-up old truck over there?"

"Yeah . . . what about it?"

"I've seen it several times before," she said. Then she went on to explain when and where. "Oh, Morgan, I know it sounds crazy, but I'm really beginning to believe whoever owns that truck has been . . . well . . . following me around and spying on me."

"But . . . why, Cat? For what purpose? You say you don't think it's anyone you know. And although you're financially well-off, you're not famous, by any means. So it's hard to imagine you'd be a candidate for kidnapping. Nor are you hiding any skeletons in your closet—at least, so far as I'm aware. So that presumably lets out blackmail, too."

"Maybe the guy's a nut case, a—a stalker!"

"Uh-huh. That's what you thought about me at first, remember? Still, I'd rather be safe than sorry. To be honest, there's something familiar about that truck. I could swear I've seen it before, too." He pulled his fountain pen and one of his business cards from his pocket. Turning the card over and cupping it against his palm, he wrote down the license-plate number of the vehicle. "Monday morning, I'll call a friend of mine at the DMV, see what I can find out. All right?"

"Yes, thanks. I'd appreciate that."

They continued on to the Cowboy, where the bouncer at the door greeted Morgan by name. The place was jampacked with people and rowdy with music, noise and laughter. Fortunately, because Morgan was tall, he could see over the crowd. After a moment, he located a couple of tables full of employees of the One-Eyed Jacks Oil & Gas Company. Taking Cat's elbow, he steered her deftly through the throng—giving more than one man who stared at her appreciatively a sharp, warning glance that clearly said, "Back off, boys. She's with me and is going to stay that way." It was all Cat could do not to laugh as each man warily sized Morgan up and then turned away, plainly deciding against tangling with his six feet, two inches of lean, hard muscle. Other men he knew he greeted boisterously, shaking their hands and clapping them on the shoulders before, with obvious pride, he introduced Cat to them. All of them paid her flattering, if outrageous and a trifle embarrassing, compliments, the kind Morgan was prone to make himself, so she understood that, as her father had been and as Morgan himself was, his friends were all reckless, rambunctious good ole boys, outlaws at heart.

"I don't think I've ever seen so many Stetsons, jeans and boots all in one place before," Cat commented, "or been called a 'filly' so many times in one night, either. In fact, I don't ever remember anybody—except you, once—referring to me that way before."

Morgan chuckled. "It's those long legs of yours, dar-lin'," he asserted, still grinning. "They just naturally make a man think of a high-spirited racehorse—among other things."

"What other things?" she queried tartly, glancing up at him sideways. Somehow he had casually managed to slide his arm around her waist possessively, and his head was bent near to hers so he could hear her over the cacophony of the Oakridge Boys belting out "Elvira," while count-less pairs of hands clapped in time to the beat and equally countless pairs of boots shuffled and stamped on the dance floor. She could smell the masculine scents of soap and co-logne that emanated from his skin, feel the warmth of his body pressed close against her in the crush.

He bent his head even lower to drawl in her ear, "Well, if you absolutely insist on knowing..."

"I do."

"Things like bridling that redheaded temper of yours and riding in your saddle, sweetheart."

"Morgan McCain!" Cat exclaimed, simultaneously in-dignant and yet perversely as wrought up as a racehorse as it waited in the starting gate, adrenaline pumping wildly. He wanted to sleep with her. He had made that plain more than once—but never before so graphically, conjuring up in her mind an image of his hands tangled in her dark red hair while he rode her, his face buried against her throat, and goaded her to climax as expertly as a jockey rode a thor-oughbred, his face bent close against its windswept mane, urging it to the finish line.

"Hey, don't blame me," Morgan said impertinently. "You're the one who insisted."

"Is that what you think about me all day at the office?"

"Yeah...ain't it awful?" Before she realized what he intended, he brushed her mouth hard and swiftly with his own, then sharply pulled away. "Now, get a move on—before I have to beat the hell out one of these good ole boys for ogling you too damned lustfully!''

"Oh! You're—you're impossible!" Cat sputtered lamely.

"And don't you just love it?" Morgan retorted insolently, grinning wickedly.

She had no time to reply, for just then they reached the tables where the employees from the One-Eyed Jacks Oil & Gas Company had congregated, the Cowboy apparently being a favorite watering hole not just of Morgan's. By now Cat knew many of the men and women, and she waved and greeted them by name as they called out to her and Morgan. Drinks and chairs were quickly shifted and two additional seats dragged over from other tables so she and Morgan had a place to sit. He motioned to a nearby waitress, and minutes later Cat had a cold beer in front of her. Hot not only from the heat of so many bodies crowded together, but also from Morgan's proximity, his arm draped across the back of her chair, his hand idly playing with her shoulder, she took a long swallow of the beer. She wondered what their employees thought, seeing them together like this. Although there had been a few joking remarks at their appearance, everybody had just seemed to accept that she and Morgan were together and to think nothing more of it. This was a far cry from the looks she had got and the comments she had overheard when she had accepted Spence's proposal of marriage. She knew that more than one of his employees had gossiped that she had slept her way to the top of the import-export firm. Doubtless they had thought she had got what she deserved when Spence had fired her. Of course, Morgan had been right: she was not *his* employee, but a co-owner of the One-Eyed Jacks Oil & Gas Company. But did that really make a difference? Somehow, Cat fervently hoped that it did, because she knew Morgan was right, and that sooner or later, her will to go on resisting him would totally crumble.

"All right, all you rowdy cowboys and cowgirls," the deejay's voice called over the PA system, "it's time to take a break from all the hootin' and hollerin'. So grab the partner of your choice while we slow things down a little with Restless Heart's 'Tell Me What You Dream.'"

As the opening strains of the tune began, the saxophone wailing, Cat turned to Morgan. "Believe it or not, this is one country-and-western song I actually know—even if I *did* think it was some bluesy pop number the first time I heard it!"

"It's the saxophone and the emphasis on the drums and bass." Pushing his chair back from the table, he stood and held out his hand to her. "Time for your dancing lesson, babe."

He said it so matter-of-factly, taking her acquiescence for granted, that she was almost tempted to retort that he might have asked—and politely. But the truth was she loved this tune, and she wanted to dance to it with him. So instead, she rose without a word and let him lead her out onto the lighted dance floor beneath the mirror-covered saddle suspended from the ceiling. Moments later she was glad she had. Morgan danced divinely, with an uncanny smoothness born of his body's inherent, fluid power, grace and rhythm. Nor was there any doubt about who was leading whom, as was so often the case with some men, who hesitated to take charge on a dance floor—or anywhere else, for that matter. Morgan held her masterfully, trusting, expecting her to follow. In his arms, Cat felt as though she had been transported into a movie or a dream. She seemed to float across the dance floor, her body perfectly in tune with his as she matched him step for step. This was how it would be to make love with him, she thought, half-dazed not only from the beer she had drunk, but also by the images of him naked and poised above her that rose again in her mind.

"Cat, you can dance," he whispered in her ear, his tone both pleased and provocative.

"Yes, Morgan."

He did not speak again, but held her even tighter, his body swaying subtly, sexily against hers as they traversed the dance floor. There was not another couple there to touch them, Cat knew, and she felt the eyes of the crowd upon them, both admiring and jealous, as they moved and whirled together. Morgan's steps grew increasingly more intricate, moving beyond the two-step to an actual swing, but even when he dipped her, Cat did not stumble, her feet lighter and surer than they had ever been in her life. The music filled her being, the saxophone and Morgan himself sending a wild thrill shooting through her as she danced on in his embrace, her eyes closed, instinct alone guiding her. She was hardly aware when the strains of the song faded, segueing smoothly into another slow tune. For the first time, she knew what Eliza Doolittle had felt when she had sung "I Could Have Danced All Night" in the movie *My Fair Lady*. Cat felt as though she could have danced forever in Morgan's arms, with the lights playing about the two of them and the mirror-covered saddle shimmering above them, casting stars beneath their feet.

But at last the deejay livened the mood again with a fast, rough-and-tumble tune, and as one, by mutual, unspoken consent, Cat and Morgan left the dance floor, knowing their own mood had been spoiled by the change of tempo in the music.

"Morgan, would you mind pointing me in the direction of the cowgirls' room?" Cat asked as they returned to the table, where she picked up her leather handbag. "I need to powder my nose."

"Your nose looks fine to me. But the cowgirls' room is thataway." He pointed toward the rest rooms. "In fact, on second thought, I'll go with you. Otherwise I might wind up having to flatten one or more of the cowboys here tonight." He walked her to the door of the ladies' room, saying, "Wait here for me if you get done before I do," as he left her to head into the men's room.

Once inside the ladies' room, Cat used the toilet, then flushed it, washing and drying her hands afterward before opening her purse to search for her makeup bag. As she glanced in the mirror, she decided Morgan had lied, that she looked ghastly. But then she had hardly ever been in a bar's bathroom where the harsh lights did *not* drain every woman's face—no matter how beautiful—of color, emphasizing the dark circles under her eyes and making her resemble a week-old corpse. Cat grimaced at her reflection, then frowned as, after several minutes of rummaging through her handbag, she failed to find her makeup bag. It must have fallen out in Morgan's Bronco, she thought, sighing impatiently, annoyed at herself. That was what she got for continually forgetting to zip her purse. She left the ladies' room to find Morgan waiting for her.

"Could I have the keys to the Bronco?" she asked.

"Why? Did I dance so badly that you're planning on driving off and leaving me stranded here as punishment?"

"Don't be silly. You dance like a dream—and you know it!" she replied tartly, then went on to explain about the loss of her makeup bag.

"I'll go look for it, Cat."

"No, I'll do it. It'll only take a moment, and I could use the fresh air besides. In the meantime, why don't you go on back to the table and order me another beer? All that dancing's made me thirsty. Relax, Morgan," she insisted when he still hesitated. "I'm not going to make off with your Bronco. The parking lots are well lighted and patrolled by security, and I can take of myself, anyway. I'm used to walking around New York—and not always in broad daylight, remember?"

"All right," he agreed reluctantly at last. "But if you're not back here in ten minutes, I'm coming after you."

"It's a deal. See you in five."

He tossed her the keys to the Bronco, and after making her way through the crowd, she left the Cowboy. The night air, although indeed fresh after the smoky atmosphere of the club, was also humid, and it clung to Cat's sweating skin, making her long for a shower as she started across the parking lots toward the Bronco. As she had learned to do in New York, she walked briskly, her head up and alert, her carriage straight and purposeful, sending out the signal that she would not be an easy target. In her hand, she held Morgan's key ring so the ends of keys protruded from between her fingers, in the manner of a makeshift brass knuckles, a trick she had learned in a self-defense course she had taken some years back. Without incident, she reached the Bronco and opened the front passenger door. The vehicle's interior light came on, so she could see her makeup bag had indeed fallen out of her handbag and lay upon the floor inside. She bent to retrieve it, then rose and turned—only to find herself face-to-face with a strange man dressed in a T-shirt and jeans, and looking none too sober as his eyes raked her lewdly.

"Damn! You're a pretty piece! Hard to believe you're ole Frank's daughter—although now that I see you up close, I can tell there's a family resemblance."

"You—you knew my father?" Cat inquired, clutching her makeup bag and wondering if it or the keys would do more damage in the event she required a weapon.

"Oh, yeah, me and Frank, we was good friends." He took a long gulp from the beer bottle he carried, then wiped his mouth off with the back of his hand. "My name's Skeeter Farrell, by the way, and I'm mighty pleased to meetcha. I used to work for One-Eyed Jacks . . . that is, before McCain fired me, the no-good bastard. He didn't have no call to do that. I'd been there damned near fifteen years! But McCain cut me loose, just like I was nothin'. Frank wouldn't of done that. He would of put things right. But before I ever got a chance to talk to him, he had that heart

REBECCA BRANDEWYNE 147

attack and died. That's why I finally come to you, Ms. Devlin. I been watching you—ever since the morning I drove out to Frank's house to talk to him. That was before I learned he had keeled over dead, of course. I didn't know who you were at first. I thought you was just some young chick livin' with ole Frank. But when I heard about Frank's death, I thought maybe you'd just bought his house or somethin'. Then one day I seen you out at One-Eyed Jacks, and even though it took me a while to figger out just who you really was, I finally put two and two together after I heard tell you'd stepped into yore daddy's shoes.'' Farrell paused, taking another generous sip of his beer. Then he continued.

"It's thisaway, you see—I want my old job back, Ms. Devlin. I got to have it. Times is hard and money's tight, and nobody's hirin' at the moment, 'specially with the aircraft companies layin' folks off.''

Wichita, Cat had learned, was known as the Air Capital of the world because of all the aircraft manufacturers that had headquarters or plants in town—Boeing, Beech, Cessna and Learjet among them, not to mention all the companies that manufactured aircraft components, engines, instruments and other equipment, parts and supplies. There were also aircraft rebuilders, aircraft upholsterers, aircraft testers, aircraft brokers, aircraft charter, rental and leasing services, aircraft ferriers and transporters and upward of a dozen aircraft schools. More than a few movie and rock stars had learned to fly in Wichita or had bought a plane there. And whenever something happened that affected the aircraft industry for the worse, Wichita's entire economy suffered.

"Look, I'd like to help you, Mr. Farrell. Really, I would,'' Cat declared placatingly. "But I'm afraid I'm not in a position to override Mr. McCain's authority at One-Eyed Jacks.''

"Why not?" he demanded, his eyes narrowing and an ugly note creeping into his voice. "Frank left you his shares in the company, didn't he? Leastways, that's what I heard through the grapevine. So you got the same rights as McCain then. You can put me back on the payroll if you wanna."

"No, I can't. Really. Now, if you'll excuse me—"

"No, I *won't* excuse you, Ms. High-'n'-Mighty Devlin! 'Cause I think you're just feedin' me a line of bull, that's what! I seen you tonight at the Cowboy, dancin' with McCain. And if he ain't already inside them sweet britches of yore'n, I'll eat my hat! So the way I figger it is this—all you gotta do is tell him you've rehired me, and it'll be a done deal."

"I'm sorry. I can't. Now I really do have to go—"

"You're not goin' anywhere, you red-haired witch—leastways, not until you either gimme my job back or gimme what you're givin' McCain." With those menacing words, Farrell abruptly flung his beer bottle away, smashing it loudly upon the pavement of the parking lot and causing Cat to jump, startled. Then, before she could collect her wits to defend herself, he grabbed her and forced her backward into the Bronco, the passenger door of which still stood open.

Despite how she struck out at him wildly with both her makeup bag and the key ring she held, scratching and bloodying his weaselly face, Farrell finally managed to compel her down onto the seat by first slapping her hard and then imprisoning her wrists. The next thing Cat knew, he was pressing his slobbering mouth to her throat and tearing roughly at her shirt and jeans. She tried to scream, but he pressed his lips over hers, cutting off the sound. After that, she saved her breath, knowing she needed it for the violent struggle she was waging against him. The longer and harder she fought, the more likely it was that the security patrol or Morgan would come.

At last she somehow got her knee up and slammed it viciously between Farrell's thighs. He half slid, half staggered backward from the Bronco into the parking lot, doubled over and groaning with pain, and as Cat rose shakily, it was to see Morgan towering above Farrell. Morgan's dark visage was terrifyingly murderous as he caught her assailant by the shoulder, jerked him up, spun him around and socked him square in the face. Cat heard the sickening sound of bone and cartilage crunching and saw blood spurt from Farrell's broken nose as he flew backward, to sprawl upon the pavement. Fear glittered in his beady eyes, but his instinct for self-preservation drove him to scramble to his feet and, with his fists, swing out at Morgan wildly. Morgan deftly sidestepped the blows, then set about to give Farrell a thrashing he would not soon forget—one that demonstrated to Cat why Morgan had been hauled away to jail for brawling in the past. She thought it was a miracle he did not beat Farrell to death, even after the man snatched up the jagged-edged neck of his broken beer bottle and slashed out with it brutally before Morgan kicked the improvised weapon from his hand.

Fortunately, however, it seemed Morgan was not so hotheaded that he did not know when to quit. Farrell was still alive, bleeding and moaning amid the shattered glass and the spilled beer upon the pavement, when Morgan finally stepped back, ending the fight and glaring down at him furiously.

"You ever, *ever* touch her again and I'll kill you, you son of a bitch!" Morgan snarled. Then he bent to retrieve his keys from where they had fallen to the ground during Cat's struggle with Farrell. "You okay?" he asked Cat tersely. Trembling, clutching her torn knit shell to her breasts, her eyes huge in her ashen face, she nodded wordlessly, fighting to hold back the sobs that rose in her throat. "Put your feet back in the Bronco, honey. I'm taking you home—and

I want to get out of here before the security patrol shows up. This is one night I don't intend to spend in jail."

"What about—what about him?" She nodded toward Farrell as she settled herself inside the vehicle and, with trembling hands, fastened her seat belt.

"I'll call him an ambulance," Morgan replied curtly, his voice hard.

"Don't...do me...any favors, McCain!" Farrell hissed between rasps for breath.

"Suit yourself." Shrugging, Morgan slammed Cat's door, then strode around the Bronco to slide in beside her. Shoving the key into the ignition, he started up the engine, tires burning rubber as he stepped on the accelerator and wheeled the Bronco from the parking lot. Turning left on Douglas, he sped along the downtown's main street, running more than one yellow light as he did so.

"Morgan, please slow down. You're angry, you're driving too fast and you're not wearing your seat belt," Cat said quietly.

At her words, he abruptly turned the Bronco down a side street, veered over to the curb and pulled to a halt, killing the motor. By then, Cat was so rattled that she burst into tears. Beside her, Morgan growled an imprecation before he unhooked her seat belt and drew her into his arms, cradling her head against his broad chest.

"Shh," he murmured, stroking her hair gently. "Hush now. Don't cry, darlin'." As he held her in his embrace, he noticed for the first time that the knit shell she wore was torn. He swore again softly. "That bastard! I should have killed him!"

"No...I'm—I'm all right. Really, I am."

"Then tell me why in the hell Farrell was trying to rape you, damn it!"

"He was drunk. Somehow he'd—he'd learned who I was—"

"Yeah, he's the one who's been following you, Cat. That battered old pickup truck you pointed out to me earlier belongs to him. That's why it looked so familiar to me."

"Oh, God... He's been spying on me off and on ever since I came to town, trying to find out all about me and—and working up his nerve to approach me. He said he used to be employed at One-Eyed Jacks before you—you fired him—"

"That's right. He was, and I did. He'd always had something of a problem with booze, but he'd managed somehow to keep it under control until recently, when his wife finally divorced him, and it became clear to me he was drinking on the job. He wouldn't admit he was an alcoholic and agree to treatment and counseling, as I advised, so I had to let him go, Cat. Machinery of any kind always poses a potential hazard, and I couldn't have him working the wells and lines, possibly endangering himself or other employees."

"No, of course not," Cat agreed. "But he's—he's terribly angry about your firing him, Morgan. He wanted me to give him his job back, and when I told him I couldn't, he turned mean and ugly. He said he'd seen us dancing together tonight at the Cowboy and that I must be...sleeping with you. And then he—he told me I was either going to rehire him or—or give him what I was giving to—to you. That's when he went berserk and attacked me."

"Well, you don't have to worry about him anymore. After tonight, he won't be bothering you again, I guarantee it."

"Maybe not, but...shouldn't we at least notify the police, Morgan? I mean, what if Farrell's crazy enough to try something else?"

"Like what? The man's a coward, Cat. Only look how long it took him to screw up his courage to approach you—and most of that, he undoubtedly got from a bottle. No, I think we can probably forget about Skeeter Farrell. He had his chance, and he blew it. But . . . damn it, Cat! When you saw he was drunk and what kind of mood he was in, why didn't you just promise him his job back, then tell me what had happened so I could deal with him?''

"I—I don't know. It all happened so fast that I—I just didn't think. And if you dare say one word about women and their emotions and their being unable to handle a tough situation as well as a man, I'll—I'll get out of this car and walk home!''

"Not down here, you won't. This area's a haven for bums and winos—not to mention hot-rodding teenagers on Friday nights. Besides, I wasn't going to say anything of the sort. Look, Cat, men and women just think differently, and that's a fact. But that doesn't make one way right or even better and the other way wrong. And there are plenty of emotional men, just as there are an equal number of cool-headed women.''

"I just don't happen to be one of the latter, right?''

"No, that's not what I'm saying at all. I'm saying every-body's different, and every situation's different, and no-body's behavior is one-hundred-percent predictable or correct one hundred percent of the time. When you thought I was a stalker, you kept your wits and coldcocked me just as cool as you please. And tonight you fought back long and hard enough to save yourself until help could arrive. Neither of those actions was the mark of a woman who can't think on her feet, babe—even if you *are* an emo-tional female. No, don't go getting all riled up on me now. I just meant you feel things deeply, Cat . . . here.'' He laid his hand gently against her heart. "I think you always have and probably always will. It's why in the hell you're weighing yourself down about it by lugging around that gigantic chip on your shoulder that's got me stymied.''

Cat could not help but laugh at that. "I suppose you'd like to knock it off, huh?''

"Among other things," Morgan uttered softly, his hands cupping her face, his thumbs tracing the tracks of her tears and brushing them away.

"Oh, no, you don't. After what you said in the Cowboy, I wouldn't touch that line again with a ten-foot pole."

"Is that so? Then I guess I'll just have to show you instead of tell you what I meant," he murmured huskily before he tipped her face up to his and his lips claimed hers, tenderly at first, then more insistently when she did not resist.

She had wanted him to kiss her, Cat realized, to take away the memory of Farrell holding her down and pressing his mouth to hers. As though he sensed her desire, her need, Morgan went on kissing her, his tongue following the contours of her lips, leaving them hot and moist before he parted them to seek the sweetness inside. Lingeringly, he tasted her, explored her, deepening the kiss until Cat moaned low in her throat, heat and longing suffusing her body. Her heart beat fast as her hands crept up to twine about his neck, to caress the thick hair that curled at the edge of his collar. Morgan's own hands still held her face, his fingers wrapped in the strands of hair at her temples as he slanted his mouth over hers, then kissed her cheek, her throat, before at last reluctantly drawing away, much to her disappointment.

"It's getting late, and the weather's starting to act up besides. See that off in the distance?" Morgan pointed to a sudden, wild barrage of flashes that lit the horizon of the night sky. "That's heat lightning. Be some hours or even days before a storm breaks, though. Still, I expect we'd better go."

Not trusting herself to speak, Cat nodded, slowly refastening her seat belt while he hooked his own into place, then started the Bronco. After pulling away from the curb, he made a U-turn in the side street to take them back out onto Douglas, where he headed east again, toward Vickridge. Within minutes, he was turning into the half-circle drive before the house that had belonged to Frank Devlin and that was now Cat's own. Morgan walked her up to the front porch bracketed by a pair of big, brass coach-lantern lights that had come on electronically when darkness had fallen. Taking her key from her outstretched hand, he unlocked the door for her and opened it.

"Do you want me to come inside with you, Cat?"

She wanted desperately to say yes, but instead, she shook her head. "No, I...I think I'd just like to take a shower and then to go to bed, if you don't mind. I'm sorry Farrell wound up spoiling our evening. It was wonderful up until then."

"Yes, it was—and it's all right, I understand about the rest. Good night then."

"Good night, Morgan."

Reaching out with one hand, he caught hold of her nape and gently pulled her to him, kissing her once more as he had done earlier in the Bronco, leaving Cat flushed and weak in the knees when he finally released her—and very much aware of his desire.

"You sure you won't change your mind about my coming inside?" he asked softly.

"No," she whispered, shaking her head.

"No, you're not sure, or no, you won't change your mind?"

"No, I'm...I won't change my mind."

"Well, I won't say I'm not disappointed. But lock up behind me then, and don't forget to set the alarm."

"I will. I won't. Thank you for the dinner and dancing, Morgan."

"Anytime, darlin'."

Whistling softly, melodically, his hands in the pockets of his jeans, he strolled toward the Bronco. It was not until Cat had closed the door behind him and turned the dead bolt that she realized the song he had been whistling was Restless Heart's "Tell Me What You Dream."

Twelve

Heat Lightning

Hearing again—although now only in her mind—the saxophone wailing bluesily, remembering how she and Morgan had danced so divinely together to the song, Cat was tempted to open the door and call him back. But in the end, she did not. Instead, after setting the alarm, she trudged slowly upstairs, vividly and uncomfortably conscious of the bigness, the emptiness of the house. With over ten thousand square feet, it really was much too large for one person, although she understood why her father had bought it. It had served as a tangible symbol of his success. But just now she would have given anything to have someone with whom to share the huge house, so it would not be so lonely. And if she were honest with herself, she knew she wanted that someone to be Morgan. Why had she let him go? Had he not already complicated her life? Did he not already haunt her restless dreams at night? So what did further in-

volvement with him matter? He was not Spence; he had
told her as much. Could she not put aside her doubts and
believe that, trust that their personal relationship would not
interfere with their professional one? She could, she
knew—and how much she wanted to do just that, how
much she wanted him. But it was too late now to change her
mind. He had already gone.

Upstairs, she undressed, throwing her torn shirt into the
wastebasket, knowing that even if it could be repaired, she
would never want to wear it again. Skeeter Farrell had put
his hands upon it, upon her. After turning on the shower,
she stepped inside the tiled enclosure, soaping and scrub-
bing herself over and over until, at last, she felt clean, un-
soiled by Farrell's touch. When she was done, Cat got out
and dried herself off, then donned a long, black silk negligee that felt sinful and sensuous against her naked skin. She
had just flicked off the lights and climbed into bed when the
telephone rang. She fumbled for the receiver in the darkness.

"Hello."

"You know what I think, Cat?" Morgan's voice sounded
in her ear, low and husky, like a long, slow caress along her
spine, sending a shiver of excitement and anticipation
through her. "I think you didn't really want to be alone
tonight. I think you didn't really want me to go. And so
now I'm wondering what you'd do if I came back. Cat?
Cat . . . are you still there? Yes, you are. I know you are. I
can hear you breathing. It makes me imagine how you'd
sound, lying naked against my chest after we'd made
love. . . . Cat?"

"I've . . . I've already locked up the house for the night,"
she told him softly, breathlessly, for the picture he evoked
in her mind was so strong, so enticing that she longed for
it to become a reality, no matter the consequences.

He laughed throatily. "I have a key, remember? After
that first night, when you mistook me for a burglar and,

with that vase, cracked me over the head, then called the police, you never did ask me for my set of your father's keys. I reckon that in all the excitement, you just forgot about 'em.''

"Yes, I did. But it doesn't matter. You see, I've already set the alarm, too.''

He laughed again, in the same soft, sexy way as before.

"Do you think I don't know the code to deactivate it, Cat? You're wrong. I do—because I'm sure you never gave a thought to changing it.'' He paused for a moment, allowing her to absorb that fact. Then he continued. "Are you already in bed, too?''

Cat knew she should deny she was, that she should lie and say she was still up and dressed. But somehow her mouth seemed to have a will of its own, refusing to cooperate with her brain.

"Yes... I'm already in bed, too.'' Was that really her own voice, so hushed, so sensuous, so tremulous with anticipation and arousal? Her hand trembled on the receiver. Her heart beat fast in her breast. Her entire body felt like molasses melting over a fire, languorous, suffused with a slow-rising, spreading heat.

"What are you wearing?'' Morgan asked hoarsely.

"A silk negligee.''

"Nothing else, Cat?''

"No.''

"What color is it?''

"Black.''

His ragged, harshly indrawn breath grated in her ear, sending another shudder through her. She knew without asking that he was envisioning her as she lay in her bed, naked save for the black silk negligee that, like a cocoon, enwrapped her body, contrasting starkly with her porcelain skin, her dark red hair, loose and tumbled about her. She knew that, as she was, he was imagining himself coming into her bedroom, undressing and sliding nude into the

bed to take her in his arms, to strip her negligee from her
body.

"If I come over, let myself in, will you still be upstairs in
bed, Cat, waiting for me? Will you?"

After a taut, provocative, seemingly interminable moment of silence, she answered.

"Yes, I will."

"I'm on my way."

The line went abruptly dead. Cat's hand was still shaking as she placed the receiver back in the cradle. She must
be out of her mind, she thought. What had she done? Was
this not how her disastrous affair with Spence had begun—with her giving in to him, against all her better judgment? She should turn on the lights, rise from her bed and
get dressed at once so she could meet Morgan at her front
door, explain she had made a mistake, had changed her
mind. Instead, she continued to lie there in darkness broken only by the silver moonlight that filtered in through the
half-open louvers of the plantation shutters screening her
bedroom windows. The pounding of her heart had not
slowed. The heat permeating her body had not dissipated.
Cat felt as though she were burning up with fever, that only
the coolness of the sheets was keeping her from bursting
into flame and melting. She almost got up to lower the
thermostat on the central air-conditioning, because the air
inside the house seemed as sultry and oppressive as that
outside. But a perverse combination of lethargy and nervous suspense held her where she lay. She wished it would
rain, but she knew from what Morgan had told her earlier
that the lightning that flashed intermittently in the distance was only heat lightning, that any storm, if it broke,
was hours or even days away. So she lay in the silence, her
ears straining to discern the purring of the Bronco's engine, and waited.

But she heard nothing beyond the sounds of the night,
for Morgan was not in his Bronco. Such were the images of

Cat that had played in his mind that, after hanging up the telephone, he had grabbed up his set of Frank's keys and headed on foot from the town house. Earlier, upon returning home, he had changed into a T-shirt and sweatpants. Now he jogged along the winding streets of Vickridge, his way lighted by the streetlights, the moonlight and the occasional bursts of lightning on the horizon. The air was so muggy that for all his excellent physical shape, he was having difficulty breathing as he ran. Still, he did not slow his pace.

Within ten minutes, he had reached Frank's house... Cat's house now—and she was upstairs, waiting for him, already in bed and wearing nothing but a black silk negligee. Morgan's groin tightened at the thought. The brass, coach-lantern lights on either side of the front door of the stately Tudor house still glowed in the darkness, making it easy for him to find the proper key on the ring he withdrew from an inside pocket. He was still panting from his run as he unlocked the door and opened it.

Upstairs, Cat heard the click of the dead bolt turning, of the door swinging open, so the distant rumble of thunder sounded louder than before. *Morgan was here!* He was actually here, inside the house! But...how? She had not heard his Bronco. He must have jogged over. Oh, God, what if it was not really him? What if it was a burglar—or, worse, Skeeter Farrell, come to finish what he had started in the Old Town parking lot? No, her highly strung nerves were causing her imagination to run wild. Of course it was Morgan. Even now she could hear the chime of the alarm as it was deactivated—and no one else but she and Morgan knew the proper code sequence to enter. But maybe whoever was downstairs had not needed the code. Maybe he had located the main box of the alarm system, somehow knocked out its power.... Scenes from every thriller she had ever watched at the movies or on TV or read in a book rose in her mind to haunt her. No, she reassured herself again, she was being silly. It was Morgan bounding so quickly and lightly up the stairs, his every breath a serrated rasp cutting the silence sharply. The next thing she knew, his tall, dark, silhouetted figure was looming in the doorway of her bedroom. She could not see his face.

"Morgan?" she whispered hesitantly, half frightened, half exhilarated, her heart thudding so hard that she thought it would burst. "Morgan?"

He did not answer. Instead, he prowled toward her, moving deeper into the shadows, ripping his T-shirt off over his head as he came, carelessly throwing it aside. Lifting first one foot and then the other, he yanked off his sneakers, not even bothering to untie them, and his socks, dropping them behind him. Then he stepped from his sweatpants and briefs. Naked, he stood at the edge of the bed, staring down at her.

Cat was everything Morgan had ever imagined, lying there, waiting for him, the diffuse moonlight dancing over her, its silvery glow making her appear like some other worldly enchantress. Her hair looked as though it were aflame, a fiery halo about her head. Her skin gleamed as white and lustrous as a pearl. The black silk negligee she wore was so understated in its elegance that he knew how expensive it must have been. It had spaghetti straps, one of which had slipped from her shoulder, and a heart-shaped bodice cut in a deep V that bared the generous swell of her full breasts, which rose and fell shallowly and as swiftly as the pulse at the hollow of her graceful throat. From its bodice, the negligee continued like a sheath to her ankles. Beginning at the front of the hem, a long slit that reached nearly to her thighs exposed a tantalizing glimpse of her long, racy legs. Morgan had, in his time, seen garments a hell of lot more revealing, but they, and the women in them, had been nothing to compare to Cat in the black silk negligee. He thought she was the sexiest female he had ever seen, and for a moment he was half-afraid he was no going to be able to hold back, that he was going to be finished before he even got started. With iron control, he mastered himself and slipped beside her into the bed.

"Morgan...?" Cat murmured uncertainly once more as his weight sank upon the mattress, the word dying upon her lips, swallowed by his carnal mouth, which without warning seized her own ravenously, devouring her.

She did not ask again, but gave herself up to him as his hands burrowed roughly through her hair, tightening at her temples and pulling her face up to his. He ground his mouth against hers, his mustache grazing her, his teeth nibbling her lower lip before his tongue traced its outline, then plunged deep inside her mouth to tangle and twine with her own tongue. Such were the sensations and emotions Morgan evoked inside her that Cat was not even aware of how her hands had crept up his chest to tunnel through his own hair, to draw him even nearer as she kissed him back with spiraling passion, low whimpers emanating from her throat, spurring him on.

After long minutes during which she ached to feel her skin totally naked and pressed against his, Morgan's hands slid down to her shoulders, tugging the thin straps of her negligee from her arms to bare her breasts. Then, as though he, too, had hungered for their flesh to meet, he crushed her to him, his head buried against her throat, his mouth gently biting the soft, vulnerable spot where her shoulder joined her nape. Like the heat lightning that shattered the night sky beyond the bedroom windows, electricity jolted through her so her back arched, causing her swollen breasts to rub sensuously against his broad chest. He groaned, long and low, his breath hot upon her skin before his tongue darted forth to lick and tease the tiny pulse that jerked erratically at the hollow of her throat. That and the way in which the dark hair that matted his chest brushed the sensitive peaks of her breasts tortured Cat so exquisitely that she was nearly half-mad with desire. Her hands clutched

Morgan's back, slick and sheened with sweat in the aftermath of his jog. Her nails dug into his flesh as, at the secret heart of her, the spark he had ignited with his kisses
caught flame, searing her.

But although she pressed against him suggestively, so she
could feel the hardness of his arousal against her at the
juncture of her thighs, he restrained himself, ignoring her
silent plea. Instead, his palms glided down to cup her
breasts, his thumbs skimming her flushed nipples, rotating
slowly, tauntingly, across them. From their tips, pleasure
radiated through her in waves that rippled clear to her toes,
curling them. But even that reaction paled in comparison
to what she felt when, after a moment, Morgan pressed her
breasts high, then lowered his head and slowly drew one
taut, tingling peak into his mouth, sucking hard. In that
moment, Cat ceased to think; she could only feel, becoming a quivering mass of all-consuming sensation. His teeth
captured her nipple, holding it in place for the flicking and
laving of his tongue as she strained and moaned against
him. Her hands, fingers tensed and splayed, moved down
his back and buttocks, searching out responsive spots,
rubbing and kneading, eliciting another groan from him.
His lips scalded the valley between her breasts. His tongue
snaked out and, with a long, languorous lick, lapped away
the sweat that trickled there before his mouth took possession of her other breast, torturing it as sweetly as he had its
twin.

Cat felt as though for the first time in her life she was
learning what it was to be seduced by a man. That Morgan
still had not spoken, that, in some dark corner of her mind,
the tiniest bit of doubt remained about his identity, only
added spice and excitement to their lovemaking, giving it a
sense of the forbidden, the dangerous. He was big and
strong. She could feel his muscles quivering and bunching
in his back as he embraced her, his arms like a pair of steel
bands imprisoning her, although she was a willing captive.

Yet for all his power, all his sensual savagery, his torment of her bore an unmistakably tender edge, so she knew he was aware of her not just as a woman, but also as a person. That this night, this joining, had more meaning for him than just an assuagement of his lust.

That realization, too, heightened the intensity of Cat's feelings, her desire, her longing. She wanted Morgan desperately, had wanted him from the very beginning, she realized, when she had first seen him striding toward her on that dusty country road. She had never before known a man such as he, a man who teased and aroused her as he did, taking his own sweet time with her, despite the fact that his labored breathing told her how he hungered for her, ached for her, as she ached for him.

His mouth claimed hers again with an urgency that sent another electric thrill coursing through her. His tongue plunged deep between her lips, seeking, finding, tasting her as though she were warm honey that trickled enticingly upon his tongue and he could not get enough of her. Her hands moved upon him restlessly. Her fingers tangled in his thick, glossy hair, curled around her neck, crept down to brush the fine, damp strands that dusted his chest, to explore the planes and angles of his body, to trace the outline of muscle and sinew. His sweating flesh was like raw silk beneath her palms, like the sensuous feel of her negligee caressing her own skin as Morgan reached down to push the fabric up about her thighs so the slit in the front of the garment both framed and revealed her womanhood. His hand trailed lingeringly down her belly, coming to rest upon the soft, hidden petals of her. He touched her there, a quick, light stroke that was sweet, wild agony to her. Cat gasped and moaned against his mouth, arched wantonly against his hand. She was fire and ice, burning and melting, helpless against the exigent, instinctive need for fulfillment that had seized her.

This time he did not ignore her imploring whimpers, but slid his fingers deep into the well of her carmine softness, only to withdraw them tormentingly, spreading quicksilver heat, before slipping them into her again. His thumb parted the cleft of her, discovering the key to her pleasure, circling and fondling until she was frantic, nearly sobbing for release. And all the while, his fingers taunted her, and he kissed her, his tongue mimicking the movements of his hand. Cat clutched him fiercely, her nails raking his back as she sought to drag him onto her.

"Please..." she entreated softly, hoarsely. "I want you, Morgan...all of you. I need to feel you inside of me...now...."

He rolled atop her then, suddenly and roughly in his urgency, his need, his hands beneath her knees, spreading her wide for him as, with a low, tortured groan, he drove into her, sure and hard and deep, taking her breath as he filled her. With a gasp, a cry, she arched her hips to receive him, meeting each strong thrust as he moved within her, taking her to the heights of rapture. She clung to him tightly as the tremors built inside her, rocked her violently with their explosion before Morgan's own release came. He shuddered long and hard against her, his face buried against her shoulder, his breath hot upon her slick, dewy skin.

After a while he withdrew from her, turning to lie upon his back and pulling her into his embrace, cradling her against his chest. She could feel his heart pounding as furiously as her own, could hear the rasp of his breath against her ear.

"Morgan?" she whispered.

He laughed, the sound low and wicked with humor.

"What if I told you I wasn't your Morgan, Cat?" he drawled teasingly as he stroked her dark red hair possessively. "That'd be quite a shock to your senses, I would imagine...finding out you'd just made love to a total stranger."

"Is that why you wouldn't answer me...so I'd think you *were* a stranger? I'll admit I did wonder at first, and it *was* exciting, that tiny bit of doubt. But when you kissed me, I knew it was you. So tell me, are you...*my* Morgan, I mean?" Her fingers traced tiny circles and spirals amid the fine hair on his chest.

"If you want me to be."

"I think perhaps I do, you know."

"You *think*?" he rejoined dryly. "What do you mean...you *think*?"

"Well, I haven't quite made up my mind yet. You're going to have to make love to me again before I can decide. You see, I'm afraid the first time was so incredible that I was completely dazed all through it. Next time, I'll have better control of myself, so I'll be in a better position to judge your worth as a lover." A smile tugged at the corners of her lips.

"Oh, you will, will you? Well, we'll just have to see about that, won't we? Come here, you." He tightened his hold upon her, turning her over upon her back, his mouth descending to cover hers in the darkness. "God, how I've wanted you, Cat," he muttered against her lips, "and yet now that you're mine, it seems I want you even more than ever before. I'm already ready and eager for you again."

"Is that so?" she inquired archly. Grasping her hand, he showed her it was indeed so, inhaling sharply when she touched him, stroked him. "What are you waiting for then?" she murmured, her breath quickening.

He laughed softly, devilishly, once more. "What's your hurry? We've got all night, don't we?"

"Yes...yes, we do," Cat agreed huskily as she wrapped her arms around his neck and drew him down to her again.

"Even so, I don't want to waste a single minute of it. Do you?"

"No…" Morgan breathed before his mouth closed over hers again, his tongue shooting deep, silencing her fiercely, feverishly, as he once more took her to paradise and back.

Thirteen

Wildcat

When Cat awoke in the morning, it was to discover she was stark naked and still lying in Morgan's embrace, in her canopy bed, which they had shared last night. He had not slipped away in the wee hours, as some men would have done, to return to his town house, but had stayed with her. She smiled drowsily at the realization, pleased by it. A man who spent the night was more serious about a relationship than one who did not. Yawning, she stirred and stretched like a sinuous cat before snuggling even closer to him.

"Hmm. That felt nice. Do that again," Morgan murmured, his eyes closed and a smile of satisfaction playing about the corners of his lips.

"You're awake!" Cat exclaimed softly.

"Barely. You wore me out last night, woman! I may never be able to get out of this bed."

"Is that so? Well, then you'll be at my utter mercy, won't you? And then I'll show you a thing or two about green-breaking a bronco," she teased.

"So show me—because if memory serves me correctly, sweetheart, for a city girl, you sure as hell know how to ride." As he spoke these last words, he glanced at her lazily, knowingly, from beneath half-closed lids, making her blush.

His hand was resting upon her breast, and now he began slowly to caress her, circling his palm lightly across her nipple. Instantly, the rosy peak contracted and stiffened in response, and a rush of heat flooded Cat's entire being. Lowering his head to her other breast, Morgan sucked its tip, his tongue flicking it until it was as taut and flushed as its twin, before, at last, he sought her mouth, kissing her deeply. With his lips and tongue and hands, he quickly brought her yearning for him to a feverish pitch before he entered her. He thrust into her once, twice. Then, crushing her to him, he suddenly rolled them both over so she was astride him. Gasping for breath, Cat gazed down at him, saw the passion that darkened his eyes, coupled with the deviltry that danced in them. He opened his mouth to speak.

"Morgan, don't even *think* about hollering, 'Ride 'em, cowgirl!'" she warned, trying without success to repress the smile that tugged at her lips at the very idea, before she began to move slowly upon him.

"I wasn't . . . going to . . . do that, darlin'."

"Yes . . . you . . . were!"

When they had finally reached their respective pinnacles and finished making love, she collapsed upon him. After a long moment, her shoulders began to shake with silent laughter.

"Confess!" she demanded, glancing up at him, laughter still bubbling in her throat. "You *were* going to say it!"

"Honey, I was not."

But Cat knew from the grin he could not hold back that she was right, that he *had* been going to say it. "You were."

"All right," he admitted sheepishly at last, still grinning. "I was, damn it! You know me too well. Will you forgive me if I fix you breakfast?"

She kissed him lightly on the nose. "Yes."

They took a long, hot shower together, Morgan thanking God that the water was steaming for a change, making Cat burst into laughter again when he told her how many cold showers he had subjected himself to over the past several weeks. He soaped her and then she soaped him, and they wound up making love again, with the warm spray from the shower head pouring upon them. After that they dressed and went downstairs. True to his word, Morgan cooked breakfast, while Cat meandered outside to fetch the morning newspaper from the driveway.

"What sections do you want?" she asked him as she slid the newspaper from the clear plastic cover that protected it in case of rain, then poured herself a cup of coffee and sat down at the kitchen table.

"Editorial, Sports and the Stock Market Report."

"Now, that's a man's combination if I ever heard one. Still, I'm afraid I'll fight you for the Stock Market Report, at least."

"No, I'll be a gentleman and let you have it first. Besides, I always read Fred Mann's sports column and Randy Brown's op-ed before I look at the Stock Market Report anyway, because I enter all the figures of the latter into my computer."

"Okay...here's Randy. Hmm. He's quite good-looking," she announced, casting from beneath long, thick lashes a surreptitious glance at Morgan as she studied Brown's picture alongside his column. She leafed through the remaining sections. "And here's Fred. My, he's handsome, too."

"If you say so, Cat. I don't read 'em for their looks. I read 'em because I happen pretty much always to agree with Fred's observations and predictions when it comes to sports, and because Randy's editorials always crack me up. Whenever this town starts filling up with hot air like a balloon, he can always be counted on to have a pin handy. One time, when all the yuppies in Tall Grass were battling a zoning change in order to prevent a Wal-Mart from being built across the street from their neighborhood, and all the equally upscale residents of Eastborough were attempting to prevent anybody from driving through their neighborhood to Towne East Mall, Randy wrote an absolutely hysterical editorial about the Balkanization of Wichita. I almost died laughing when I read it. How do you like your eggs?"

"Over easy. Well, I don't know about their columns, but if these two guys are any example of the men who work there, I believe I'll apply for a job at the *Wichita Eagle* if you wind up throwing me out of One-Eyed Jacks."

"I don't think you have to worry about that, babe." Glancing up from the stove, Morgan eyed her intently, appreciatively. "You're not only doing a great job, but I've also grown rather attached to you—besides which, you don't know anything about working for a newspaper."

"I could learn," she declared brightly.

"Now where and when did I hear that line before?" he teased. "However, after what I've seen, I no longer doubt it in the slightest. Still, you can forget it, Cat. You're not going to work anywhere but at One-Eyed Jacks, where you belong . . . with me."

"Is that so?"

"Yeah, that's so. End of discussion. Now, please give me those newspaper sections. Much as I like their columns, I *don't* like the idea of your ogling Fred and Randy over *my* breakfast!"

"That's okay. I've come to prefer a man with a mustache anyway—and neither of them has one."

"Good. I'll buy a razor then for every man you meet."

Cat laughed so hard at that that she nearly choked on her coffee. In fact, during the whole weekend, she laughed more than she could remember laughing in a long time. Morgan both made her laugh and made love to her endlessly. He returned home only once the entire weekend—to get clothes and to pick up his Bronco—and even then he took her with him, so she got to see his town house for the first time. Like her father's house when she had first moved into it, it was beautifully decorated, but obviously a man's domain, lacking a woman's touch. Unlike most bachelor pads, however, it was clean and tidy—but then Cat had expected no less from a man who sent even his jeans to the dry cleaners to be starched and pressed.

On Monday morning—later than either of them normally arrived at work—Morgan drove Cat to the offices of the One-Eyed Jacks Oil & Gas Company, insisting it was silly of them to take two cars, especially when they both lived in the same neighborhood. In the end, she reluctantly agreed, although she still wondered what their employees would think.

"Who cares what they think?" Morgan growled in response to her question. "We don't meddle in their private lives, and I don't expect them to meddle in ours."

When they entered the office, Josie, the receptionist, was already at her desk.

"Could you please hold for a moment?" she said into the telephone receiver she held to her ear. Then, punching the Hold button, she glanced up at Cat. "Cat, this is a long distance call for you . . . from New York."

"Oh, Jeez Louise, I hope it's not my mother!"

"No." Josie shook her head. "It's a man. He said his name is . . . wait just a minute, I've got it right here. . . ." From her desk, she picked up the pink telephone message slip she had begun to fill out. "His name is Spencer Kingsley. Do you want me to put him through to your office?"

For a long moment, Cat made no reply. She was shocked that Spence had tracked her down and called her. She was vividly aware of Morgan at her side, of the tension that had abruptly tautened his body at Josie's announcement, so he was like a predator preparing to spring. Cat knew he did not want her to take Spence's call. She was surprised he had not answered Josie's question himself, instructing her to inform Mr. Kingsley that Cat was not yet in. But then she recognized that, for all his seemingly macho talk and behavior, Morgan would never make her own decisions for her unless it were a matter of life and death.

"Yes, put Mr. Kingsley through to my office, Josie," Cat directed at last. Then, glancing at Morgan, she said softly, "I owe him that much, I think."

"If you say so, Cat," he replied tonelessly, a muscle flexing in his jaw, so she knew he was not as unaffected by her decision as he sought to appear. Then he went into his office and closed the door firmly behind him.

Going into her own office and shutting the door, Cat picked up the receiver of her telephone and punched the button of the blinking line.

"Hello, Spence," she said to her ex-fiancé coolly. "What can I do for you?"

They talked for a little more than half an hour. Even so, Cat had no sooner ended the conversation than Morgan appeared in her office, so she knew that all the while, he had been watching his own telephone, waiting for her to hang up and the light on the line she was using to go dark.

"So...what did your former fiancé want?" he asked casually, with just the slightest emphasis on the word *former,* his eyes hooded so she could not guess his thoughts.

"He...ah...wanted to apologize for the argument we had in Europe, the one that led to our breakup. He said he had missed me, and he asked me when I was planning on returning to New York. He intimated that since my departure from the import-export firm, things have not been going as smoothly as they did when I was there, and he offered me not only my old job back, but also a full partnership. And then he told me he would... ah... like very much to—to renew our engagement," she ended quietly.

For a moment silence stretched between them, tense and awkward.

"I see." Morgan's tone was terse. "And what was your response to all that, Cat?"

She never had a chance to reply, for just then Whitty came running into the office, visibly upset, her face stricken.

"Morgan, Quint just called," she announced agitatedly, one hand at her breast. Quint was the shop foreman. "You've got to get out to the Deuces Wild Number Seven right away. That no-good Skeeter Farrell's set it on fire— and it's burning out of control!"

"My God," Cat breathed. "Morgan, wait! I'll go with you!"

Grabbing up her purse, she ran after him as he tore out of the office and raced to the Bronco, pausing just long enough for Cat to slide in beside him as he started up the vehicle. By the time she got her seat belt fastened, he was already speeding down the street, heading north toward the city limits.

"Get Quint on his cellular," he directed tersely, a muscle working in his jaw. "Find out what in the hell happened and what's been done about it so far. Tell him we're en route, that we'll be there as soon as we can."

"Right." Cat nodded, picking up Morgan's cellular telephone and punching in Quint's number. As though he had been expecting the call, he answered almost immediately. "Quint, this is Cat. Morgan and I are on our way to the Deuces Wild. Could you fill us in on what you know and what action you've taken so far?" she asked as Morgan concentrated on driving, weaving in and out of traffic impatiently.

"Well, I don't know much, except for what I already told Whitty." Quint's voice sounded in her ear. "Because we'd been having a problem with some of the equipment, Ty Anders—he's the pumper on the Deuces Wild line—had departed from his usual routine this morning," he explained, "going straight out to Number Seven. By the time he got there, the well was already on fire, but he saw Skeeter's old pickup truck barreling away from the site. That's how come we figured Skeeter was responsible for the fire."

"How did Farrell start it?"

"Who knows? Your guess is as good as mine, Cat. A Molotov cocktail, a pipe bomb, a stick of dynamite.... Hell! He could have used most anything like that. But whatever it was, it blew the beam pump sky-high—Ty says there're pieces of it all over the place—and it set the surrounding field ablaze, too. I've notified the fire department, and they've got trucks on the way even as we speak."

"Was anybody hurt by the explosion?"

"No, although if Ty had arrived a few minutes earlier, he probably would have been killed. He was just lucky his truck had a dead battery this morning."

"Did you call the sheriff's department, Quint?"

"You betcha! They're sending officers.... We'll probably have to have some kind of bomb squad, too, if we find out Skeeter rigged more than one well to blow. I've pulled men off some of the other lines to help out."

"Good." That seemed to cover everything Cat could think of, so she hung up, then relayed all the information to Morgan.

"Quint's a good man, an excellent foreman," Morgan declared. "I feel confident he's done everything that could be done at this point and has the situation in hand. But we'll know for sure when we get to the Deuces Wild site." Without warning, he banged his fist on the steering wheel.

"Damn that Skeeter Farrell! I should have listened to you, Cat, and reported him to the police Friday night when he attacked you! I should have realized then how desperate and crazed he'd grown. Instead, I put his action down to the booze and figured that after our fight, he'd slink away with his tail between his legs and wouldn't pose a threat anymore, either to you or One-Eyed Jacks. My God! What if he hadn't chosen one of the wells as his target? What if he'd come back for you, Cat?"

"But he didn't."

"That's not the point! He might have!" Morgan's fingers clenched and unclenched around the steering wheel. "I would never have forgiven myself if Farrell had harmed you, Cat. I'm not sure he'd have survived when I'd got done with him."

"Then I'm glad I wasn't his target," Cat said, for she suspected Morgan's temper was such that he might have carried out his threat. And while it was exciting to know how deeply he cared for her and that he was more than willing to come to her defense, when she actually thought of his size and strength and remembered the thrashing he had given Farrell in the parking lot of Old Town, she shivered. It was difficult to believe the man who made love to her with such power and passion and yet such tenderness could be so lethal.

In many respects he was like a throwback to the nineteenth century. That was, Cat thought, one of his principal attractions. Now, when she recalled her arrival in Wichita, her awakening in the taxi and feeling as though she had been transported back in time, she envisioned Morgan in her mind as well. She could see him striding out of fire and smoke on the horizon of the prairie, dressed in a long duster, guns in hand.

That image became something of a reality when they finally reached the site of Deuces Wild Number Seven, where chaos reigned. Fire trucks, water trucks, sheriff's cars, One-

Eyed Jacks company trucks and other vehicles were already parked haphazardly around the location. A sheriff's
officer on the scene stopped the Bronco, but then allowed
it to pass after Morgan had identified himself and Cat.
Morgan parked the car, and the two of them got out, staring at the sight before them. A long plume of flame roared
from the well, billowing smoke into the air. The gas line had
ruptured. Fire and smoke swept across the field as well, and
it was on this that the firemen were concentrating most of
their initial efforts, lest the blaze spread to other wells or to
the storage tanks for crude oil. Water spewed from long
hoses hooked up to the water trucks. Men operating heavy
machinery were digging trenches in the distance, in prepa-
ration for starting a backfire if it became necessary.

"Wait here," Morgan ordered Cat firmly.

With a handkerchief, he covered his face against the
waves of acrid black smoke, then raced toward the burning well and Quint, who had already arrived. Standing in
the middle of the confusion, the foreman was simultaneously talking to a sheriff's officer and shouting orders to
employees of the One-Eyed Jacks Oil & Gas Company. Cat
chafed fiercely at remaining behind by the Bronco. Still, she
had sense enough to realize that, realistically, there was little she could do to help and that, as a result, she would only
be in the way if she, too, charged toward the well. Sirens
wailing, more fire trucks appeared on the scene, along with
additional water trucks. She saw one of the sheriff's officers talking into his radio, and at that, she recognized that
there was, after all, some action she could take.

Climbing back into the Bronco, she seized Morgan's cellular telephone and dialed the offices of the corporation.

"Josie, this is Cat," she said when the receptionist answered. "Put me through to Whitty immediately, please."
In seconds the secretary was on the line. "Whitty, I need
you to take whatever money you need from petty cash and
to go to a fast-food restaurant or deli or wherever you think

est. Buy enough sandwiches and chips to feed an army, and see what you can do about getting some jugs of cold lemonade and iced tea as well. Between the summer heat and the fire, it's like an inferno out here, and since the situation is awfully bad, I don't think it's going to be resolved anytime soon. I don't know how many of the men have their lunch boxes with them, if any do, or whether they have anything to drink. Turn on the answering machine, and take Josie and Grace with you if you need help.'' Grace was the general office clerk. ''Then head this way. Meanwhile, I'll call Stella at the shop and tell her to close down and meet us here. Between the five of us, we ought to be able to manage.''

''Understood,'' Whitty replied briskly. ''We're on our way.''

Thanking God that Whitty was so efficient, Cat rang off, then telephoned Stella, relaying the necessary instructions. In moments Stella, too, was en route. Once Cat had finished her calls, there seemed little else for her to do except sit and wait. More than once, she climbed into the driver's seat and started up the engine to run the Bronco's air conditioner, she was so hot and perspiring. When Morgan returned, she told him she had ordered both the offices and the shop of the One-Eyed Jacks Oil & Gas Company closed, and that Whitty, Josie, Grace and Stella were on their way with food and drink.

''Good idea, Cat. I should have thought of it myself.''

''No, you've got enough on your mind as it is, Morgan.'' She motioned toward the burning well. ''What are they going to do about that? Can the fire be put out?''

''Probably. As you've learned, wells requiring beam pumps lack sufficient pressure to force the oil to the surface—which is what necessitates the beam pump in the first place—and the output from Deuces Wild Number Seven has been steadily falling off anyway, so its resources were beginning to be exhausted. It was one of the wells I was thinking about shutting down. So now we're going to try to extinguish the fire and then seal off the well. I don't know how long that will take, however.''

In the end, it took several days to bring the fire under control, then put it out and cap off the well and the gas line as well as clean up the debris from the surrounding area. During that time, Skeeter Farrell was arrested, and evidence was discovered in his garage that, along with the pumper, Ty Anders, having witnessed him fleeing the scene of the fire, linked him definitely to the crime. Farrell was currently cooling his heels in jail, having been unable to raise the bail money he had needed to regain his freedom.

During the days that Morgan had overseen the hectic operations at Deuces Wild Number Seven, he and Cat had had little free time to spend together. Much to her disappointment, he had returned home most nights to his town house—hungry, dirty, in need of food and a shower and utterly exhausted. After calling her to bring her up to date on the status of the well and to tell her good-night, he had hung up and collapsed on his bed, falling asleep almost instantly. By mutual, unspoken agreement, both of them had deliberately avoided mentioning the subject of Spence Kingsley's telephone call to her.

But Cat had known that once the crisis was past, the topic would arise and she and Morgan must finish the conversation they had started just as Whitty had barged into Cat's office to inform them about Farrell's sabotage of Deuces Wild Number Seven. So, during the passing days, Cat had reflected long and hard about her future. She had felt no desire whatsoever to renew her engagement with Spence, and so she had told him, grasping from his dialogue that his primary interest in her had stemmed not from any real love for her, but from the fact that his import export firm was not running nearly so smoothly without her.

That he had at last recognized her capabilities had been a gratifying thought. Still, it had not made her long to return to her old job. Since she had started work at the One-Eyed Jacks Oil & Gas Company, she had not missed the import-export firm. Nor, Cat had realized with surprise, had she missed Spence, either. Her father had been right. Spence had been a charming, convenient companion who had fit in with both her crowd and her corporate aspirations. Because of that, she had convinced herself she had fallen in love with him, deliberately blinding herself to the lack of any true passion between them.

These past several days, Cat had recognized that when Spence had gone away without her on business trips, she had felt only a mild sense of relief that she would have some time to herself. Morgan's absence, however, she had felt keenly, tossing and turning alone in her bed at night, missing him lying beside her, making love to her. When he had been injured at the site of Deuces Wild Number Seven, Cat had been stricken with dread and panic until she had learned he was not seriously hurt. She had known with certainty then how much she loved him, how deeply she would regret his loss. She wanted, she had realized then, nothing more than to remain in Kansas, to spend the rest of her life with Morgan McCain.

With that thought in mind, Cat had taken special care with her appearance this evening, as well as with the supper she had offered to prepare for the two of them, feeling that with Morgan having taken her out to so many places, she at least owed him a home-cooked meal in return. He had told her he liked spaghetti, so she had fixed that, making fresh pasta and sauce, along with an Italian salad and crusty garlic bread. When Morgan arrived, just as the sun was beginning to set, he added his own contribution to the meal—a bottle of excellent Beaujolais.

They ate in the kitchen so that, through the French doors and windows that lined the back of the house, they could watch the sun go down, a flaming ball of orange that sank slowly on the western horizon.

"Sunsets are truly beautiful here," Cat uttered softly as she and Morgan cleared the table, stacking the dirty dishes in the dishwasher before sitting back down at the table, cups of espresso in hand. "And at night, you can see the stars in the sky even from the city. They've never looked so close to me before, as though I could just reach up and pluck one from the sky."

"Yeah," Morgan agreed as he sipped his espresso. "There's nothing like the night sky over the prairie." He paused for a moment, gathering his thoughts. Then he continued. "You know, Cat, you never did tell me what your answer to Spencer Kingsley was—and we need to talk about that. But before we do, I thought we might play a little game of poker."

"Poker?" she exclaimed, genuinely surprised. "What kind of poker?"

"Two-card draw."

"What's that? I don't think I've ever even heard of i' before."

Reaching into his pocket, he withdrew a box, which he opened to reveal a deck of cards. Removing them, he began to shuffle them expertly, then placed the deck before her, indicating that she should cut. Once she had done so he fanned the cards out on the table.

"Here's the deal," he announced, eyeing her intently "We'll each draw two cards and turn them faceup on the table. If, by some chance, you happen to turn up the two one-eyed jacks, I'll give you the two percent of my stoc that Frank left me, so we'll be equal partners in the company. If, on the other hand, I happen to draw the two one eyed jacks, then instead of returning to New York to marr Spencer Kingsley, you'll agree to remain in Wichita... t marry me," he ended quietly.

"M-m-marry you? Did you say... *marry* you, Morgan?"

"*I* didn't stutter, did I? That's the bet, Cat. Are you in or out?"

She was so astounded by his proposal that she was momentarily speechless. Of course she had fantasized about him asking her to marry him. She had even dared to hope that he might, in time. But she had not expected it to happen so soon, if at all. Her heart thrummed with nervous excitement in her breast. Her hands began to tremble. What if, by some miracle, *she* drew the two one-eyed jacks and he did not? What if neither of them did?

"What—what if neither of us gets the pair of one-eyed jacks?"

Morgan shrugged. "Then the high card wins, and the loser can fix breakfast in the morning. So what do you say, Cat? Here's your chance to get your fair share of the company... *or*—" he grinned at her insolently "—me as a husband. Is it a bet?"

"Yes... yes, it's a bet."

"Then take your best shot, darlin'." He nodded at the cards on the table.

Slowly, her pulse racing, Cat reached out and pulled two cards from the deck.

"Aren't you going to look at 'em?" Morgan inquired, quirking one brow upward.

She shook her head. "Not until you pick yours."

"All right." Swiftly, hardly even glancing at the deck, he, too, drew two cards.

Only then did Cat turn hers over, gasping when she saw that, incredibly, she had drawn the pair of one-eyed jacks.

"That's—that's unbelievable! Do you know what the odds of that are?"

"Yeah, I do. Looks like you'll be getting my stock... *and*—" he turned his own two cards faceup, grinning impudently again "—marrying me, too, sweetheart."

For a long moment Cat stared at his own pair of one-eyed jacks, stunned. Then she realized what he had done, and, her heart pounding harder than ever, she began to turn all the cards over.

"I hadn't a chance at losing, had I? And neither did you, Morgan! They're all one-eyed jacks . . . all the cards! You rigged the deck! You cheated!"

"Yeah . . . but you know what they say—all's fair in love and war. And I *do* love you, Cat." His dark visage softened as he looked at her, his eyes smoldering with desire like twin embers and shining unmistakably with love. His voice was husky with emotion. "The day you came into it was the best day of my entire life. I don't want to lose you, darlin'. Please say you'll stay. Say you'll marry me."

"Yes . . . and again, yes. Oh, Morgan!" Her eyes filled with sudden tears of happiness as she gazed at him. "I love you, too!"

Standing, he swept her up into his arms, kissing her fiercely and deeply as he began to carry her toward the front staircase, which led upstairs, to her bedroom. Clinging tightly to his neck, Cat kissed him back with equal fervor, sure in her heart that, this time, she was feeling that certain special something with a certain special someone. This time she was sure beyond a shadow of a doubt that she had got it right. As though in answer to her thoughts, she seemed to hear from the study, as Morgan bore her past it, the echo of her father's laughter and then the smug, pleased sound of his voice.

My two wildcats—together at last!

Thanks, Dad, she called silently over her shoulder before tightening her hold on Morgan and smiling up at him invitingly, her heart in her eyes. "Well, I suppose this filly's about to be roped and branded permanently!" she said.

"Why, of course, darlin'," Morgan drawled wickedly, his eyes dancing as he carried her down the hallway and into her bedroom. "Don't you know? I've already got my lariat stashed and waiting under your bed!"

She laughed joyously, her heart singing as he tossed her down on the bed, then fell upon her to gather her into his strong and loving arms—then and for always.

Epilogue

The Winning Hand

He ought to have had the flowers delivered, Morgan thought ruefully as he strode through the maze of corridors in HCA Wesley Hospital, his vision almost totally obscured by the huge crystal vase filled nearly to overflowing with beautiful mixed flowers—Cat's favorite kind of arrangement—that he carried. But he had wanted to bring the bouquet himself, along with the big stuffed Teddy bear he had securely tucked under one arm, and the Wranglers baseball cap he had crammed in the back pocket of his jeans.

After an elevator trip and some more long halls, Morgan finally reached Cat's private room in the maternity ward. There, he awkwardly shifted his burdens so he could knock softly on the door. Then, with his shoulder, he pushed open the heavy wooden door and tiptoed inside the room, managing to peek through the towering flowers to see if his wife was asleep. To his delight, she was awake, her hospital bed cranked up so that she was in a sitting position and their newborn son, Frank Devlin McCain, cuddled snugly against her breast. Morgan thought he had never seen her look so beautiful. In the golden sunlight that streamed in through the open blinds of the window, her skin positively glowed in that luminescent way that was peculiar to new mothers, and her dark red hair shone like fire opals.

Spying her husband, Cat's eyes lit up warmly with love, and she smiled with pleasure before holding one finger warningly to her lips.

"Shh," she whispered, glancing down tenderly at their baby. "He's just now finished his feeding and dropped off to sleep." She motioned toward her hospital table. "Set those gorgeous flowers down there before you drop them, Morgan, then wheel that table a little closer so I can see them, please."

"As you wish," he replied, grinning and causing her both to smile again and to blush at the memories that his words evoked. On the evening that they both felt certain that little Frank had been conceived, they had rented a movie, *The Princess Bride,* and watched it together before making love passionately and tenderly long into the night. Ever since then, Morgan had taken to saying teasingly the film's famous line, "As you wish," to Cat's every expressed desire.

He placed the flowers on the table, then moved it to the bed.

"They're just beautiful," Cat declared quietly as she touched the blossoms gently and bent her head to inhale their fragrant scent. "Thank you, my love. And now, since I have a strange, sneaking suspicion that that colossal Teddy bear is for little Frank and not for me, why don't you put it in his bassinet. Then you can kiss us both and hold him for a while."

"There's nothing I'd like better." Morgan propped the big Teddy bear up in one corner of the plastic, hospital bassinet, which one of the nurses had wheeled into the room earlier. Then he bent and kissed his wife lingeringly before taking little Frank into his arms. "Come here, Ace," he said as lifted the sleeping baby, cradling him gingerly.

"Morgan—" Cat eyed him with mock reproval, trying but failing to repress her rueful smile "—I thought we had agreed our son would *not* be called Ace, Deuce, Trey, Jack, King, or any other name connected in any way, shape, or fashion with cards or poker."

"I know we did, Cat. But...well, damn it! You've just got to trust me on this one. No little boy wants to go through life being called Frankie, does he, Ace?" Morgan looked down at his son, and as though in response to his father, little Frank opened his eyes drowsily, waving one tiny fist in the air before yawning widely and drifting back to sleep. "There. You see?" Morgan shot Cat a triumphant glance that quickly turned sheepish as she shook her head and rolled her eyes at him to indicate just what she thought of his perception on little Frank's "answer." "Oh, I almost forgot." Morgan hastily changed the subject, reaching into his back pocket and drawing forth the Wranglers baseball cap, which he placed gently at a cocky angle on the sleeping baby's head.

"Oh, Morgan." Cat laughed softly. "You're incorrigible!"

"Yeah, but you love it—and me."

"I do."

"Good—because I love you, too, and so I'm never going to let you get away from me. You're my queen of hearts. Between you and Ace here, I got dealt the world's winning hand." Taking the cap off little Frank and putting it on the Teddy bear's head, Morgan laid the baby tenderly in the bassinet. Then drawing one of the hospital chairs up next to Cat's bed, her husband sat down, pulling a deck of cards from his shirt pocket. "And since I feel so incredibly lucky, do you feel up to our afternoon poker game?" That was how he had been entertaining her while she was in the hospital.

"Yes. Jacks or better to open?" Cat inquired, lifting one eyebrow archly.

Morgan grinned. "As you wish," he said.

* * * * * *

COMING NEXT MONTH

#961 ANGELS AND ELVES—Joan Elliott Pickart

The Baby Bet
November's *Man of the Month*, Forrest MacAllister, is the
MacAllister clan's most confirmed bachelor, as well as its
Baby Bet Champion. But winning bets is nothing compared to
maintaining his bachelor status around sexy Jillian Jones-Jenkins!

#962 ONCE IN A BLUE MOON—Kristin James

When Michael Traynor took off years ago, Isabelle Gray swore
she'd never fall for him again. Now he was back—and she had to
keep a ten-year-old secret she'd hidden from him since he left....

#963 WHATEVER COMES—Lass Small

Sean Morant was used to having beautiful women draped on
his arm, but that was *before* he met Amabel Clayton. She was as
determined as she was feisty, and somehow Sean had to make the
stubborn woman his!

#964 COWBOY HOMECOMING—Pamela Ingrahm

Cowboy Steve Williams came home to find Tegan McReed
claiming she owned *his* land! But getting the beautiful woman
off his ranch—and his mind—wasn't as easy as it seemed!

#965 REBEL LOVE—Jackie Merritt

Cass Whitfield was devastated when Gard Sterling couldn't
even remember the wonderful night they'd spent together! Could
Gard convince her that he wasn't the same bad boy who hurt her
years ago?

#966 ARIZONA HEAT—Jennifer Greene

When Kansas McClellan asked Paxton Moore to help her find
her missing brother, she knew she was in trouble. Not only was
the man stubborn, but he was sexy enough to make her heat rise
to a dangerous level!

Take 4 bestselling love stories FREE

Plus get a FREE surprise gift!

Special Limited-time Offer

Mail to Silhouette Reader Service™

> P.O. Box 609
> Fort Erie, Ontario
> L2A 5X3

YES! Please send me 4 free Silhouette Desire® novels and my free surprise gift. Then send me 6 brand-new novels every month, which I will receive months before they appear in bookstores. Bill me at the low price of $2.74 each plus 25¢ delivery and GST*. That's the complete price and a savings of over 10% off the cover prices—quite a bargain! I understand that accepting the books and gift places me under no obligation ever to buy any books. I can always return a shipment and cancel at any time. Even if I never buy another book from Silhouette, the 4 free books and the surprise gift are mine to keep forever.

326 BPA AQS5

Name	(PLEASE PRINT)	
Address	Apt. No.	
City	Province	Postal Code

This offer is limited to one order per household and not valid to present Silhouette Desire® subscribers. *Terms and prices are subject to change without notice. Canadian residents will be charged applicable provincial taxes and GST.

CDES-295

Become a *Privileged Woman,*
You'll be entitled to all these *Free Benefits.* And *Free Gifts,* too.

To thank you for buying our books, we've designed an exclusive FREE program called *PAGES & PRIVILEGES™.* You can enroll with just one Proof of Purchase, and get the kind of luxuries that, until now, you could only read about.

Big HOTEL DISCOUNTS

A privileged woman stays in the finest hotels. And so can you—at up to 60% off! Imagine standing in a hotel check-in line and watching as the guest in front of you pays $150 for the same room that's only costing you $60. Your *Pages & Privileges* discounts are good at Sheraton, Marriott, Best Western, Hyatt and thousands of other fine hotels all over the U.S., Canada and Europe.

Free DISCOUNT TRAVEL SERVICE

A privileged woman is always jetting to romantic places. When <u>you</u> fly, just make one phone call for the lowest published airfare at time of booking— <u>or double the difference back!</u>

PLUS—you'll get a $25 voucher to use the first time you book a flight AND <u>5% cash back on every ticket you buy thereafter through the travel service!</u>

PROOF OF PURCHASE

Offer expires October 31, 1996

SD-PP67